# PRAISE FOR RICHARD MATHESON

"*I Am Legend* is the most clever and riveting vampire novel since *Dracula*. Stylish and gripping, [Richard Matheson's] stories not only entertain, but touch the mind and heart."

—Dean Koontz

"*I Am Legend* may be one of the most influential works of fantasy written in this century."

—*Fangoria #145*

"The author who influenced me the most as a writer was Richard Matheson."

—Stephen King

"One of those who have moved imaginative fiction from the sidelines into the literary mainstream. May he be writing far into the twenty-first century."

—Ray Bradbury

"Of all the many writers I've read and admired, only two have ever managed to make my knuckles turn white. Jack London is gone, but Richard Matheson, thank God, is alive and well and working."

—Loren D. Estleman

"My hat is off to the genius of this author."

—*R\*A\*V\*E Reviews*

"Matheson inspires, it's as simple as that."

—Brian Lumley

"Richard Matheson is one of the most respected living American fantasy/science fiction/horror writers.... Matheson could not write a bad book if he tried."

—*Hartford Courant*

**Books by Richard Matheson**

*The Beardless Warriors*
*Button, Button*
*Duel*
*Earthbound*
*Hell House*
*Hunted Past Reason*
*I Am Legend*
*The Incredible Shrinking Man*
*Nightmare at 20,000 Feet*
*Noir*
*Now You See It . . .*
*7 Steps to Midnight*
*Somewhere In Time*
*A Stir of Echoes*
*What Dreams May Come*

# A STIR OF
# ECHOES

## RICHARD MATHESON

**TOR®**

A TOM DOHERTY ASSOCIATES BOOK
NEW YORK

This is a work of fiction. All the characters and events portrayed in this book are either products of the author's imagination or are used fictitiously.

A STIR OF ECHOES

Copyright © 1958 by RXR, Inc., renewed 1986 by RXR, Inc.

All lines from "Chambers of Imagery" by Archibald MacLeish are reprinted by permission of the author.

A Tor Book
Published by Tom Doherty Associates, LLC
175 Fifth Avenue
New York, NY 10010

www.tor-forge.com

Tor® is a registered trademark of Tom Doherty Associates, LLC.

ISBN-13: 978-0-7653-6117-2
ISBN-10: 0-7653-6117-5

First Edition: September 1999
Second Edition: May 2008

Printed in the United States of America

0  9  8  7  6  5  4  3  2

For Chuck and Helen
with affection

Sometimes within the brain's old
ghostly house,
I hear, far off, at some forgotten
door,
A music and an eerie faint carouse
And stir of echoes down the
creaking floor.

"Chambers of Imagery"
Archibald MacLeish

# ONE

THE DAY IT ALL STARTED—A HOT, August Saturday—I'd gotten off work a little after twelve. My name is Tom Wallace; I work in Publications at the North American Aircraft plant in Inglewood, California. We were living in Hawthorne, renting a two-bedroom tract house owned by one of our next-door neighbors, Mildred Sentas. Another neighbor, Frank Wanamaker, and I usually drove to and from the plant together, alternating cars. But Frank didn't like Saturday work and had managed to beg off that particular day. So I drove home alone.

As I turned onto Tulley Street, I saw the '51 Mercury coupe parked in front of our house and knew that Anne's brother, Philip, was visiting. He was a psychology major at the University of California in Berkeley and he sometimes drove down to L.A. for weekends. This was the first time he'd been to our new place; we'd only moved in two months before.

I nosed the Ford into the driveway and braked it in front of the garage. Across the street Frank Wanamaker's wife, Elizabeth, was sitting on their lawn pulling up weeds. She smiled faintly at me and raised one white-gloved hand. I waved to her as I got out of the car and started for the porch. As I went up its two steps I saw Elizabeth struggle to her feet and adjust her maternity smock. The baby was due in about three months. It was the Wanamaker's first in seven years of marriage.

When I opened the front door and went into the living room, I saw Phil sitting at the kitchen table, a bottle of Coca Cola in front of him. He was about twenty, tall and lean, his darkish-brown hair crew-cut. He glanced in at me and grinned.

"Hi, brother man," he said.

"Hi." I took off my suit coat and hung it in the front closet. Anne met me in the kitchen doorway with a smile and a kiss.

"How's the little mother?" I asked, patting her stomach.

"Gross," she said.

I chuckled and kissed her again.

"As they say," I said, "hot enough for you?"

"Don't even talk about it," she answered.

"Okay."

"Hungry?" she asked.

"Ravenous."

"Good. Phil and I were just about to start."

"Be right with you." I washed my hands and sat down across from Phil, eyeing his blindingly green polo shirt.

"What's that for," I asked, "warning off aircraft?"

"Glows in the dark," he said.

"Helps the co-eds keep track of you at night," I said. Phil grinned.

"Now don't you two get started again," Anne said, putting a dish of cold cuts on the table.

"Whatever does you mean?" Phil said to her.

"Never mind now," she said. "I don't want any needling session this weekend. It's too hot."

"Agreed," said Phil, "needling excluded. Agreed, brother man?"

"And spoil my weekend?" I said.

"Never mind," said Anne. "I can't face that and the heat both."

"Where's Richard?" I asked.

"Playing in the back yard with Candy." Anne sat down beside me with a groan. "There's a load off my feet," she said.

I patted her hand and we started eating.

"Speaking of Candy," Anne said, "I trust you haven't forgotten the party tonight at Elsie's."

"Oh my God," I said, "I did forget. Do we have to go?"

Anne shrugged. "She invited us a week ago. That was excuse time. It's too late now."

"Confusion." I bit into my ham on rye.

"Brother man seems less than joyous," Phil said. "Elsie's shindigs no goo'?"

"No goo'," I said.

"Who is she?"

"Our next-door neighbor," Anne told him. "Candy's her little girl."

"And parties are her profession," I said. "She's the poor man's Elsa Maxwell."

Anne smiled and shook her head. "Poor Elsie," she said. "If she only knew what awful things we say behind her back."

"Dull, huh?" said Phil.

"Why talk?" I said. "Go to the party with us and see for yourself."

"I'll liven 'er up," said Phil.

* * *

A little after eight-fifteen Richard fell asleep in his crib and we went next door to Elsie's house. In most marriages you think of a couple's home as *theirs*. Not so with that house. Ron may have made the payments on it but the ownership was strictly Elsie's. You felt it.

It was Ron who answered our knock. He was twenty-four, a couple of years older than Elsie, a couple of inches taller. He was slightly built, sandy-haired with a round, boyish face that seldom lost its impassive set; even when he smiled as he did then, the ends of his mouth curling up slightly.

"Come in," he said in his quiet, polite voice.

Frank and Elizabeth were already there, Elizabeth settled on the red sofa like a diffident patient in a dentist's waiting room, Frank's thin body slouched in one of the red arm chairs. He brightened only a little when we came in, raising his bored gaze from the green rug, straightening up in the chair, then standing. I introduced Phil around.

*"Hi!"*

I glanced over and saw Elsie peering around the corner of the kitchen doorway. She'd cut her dark hair still shorter and bobbed it still tighter, I noticed. When we'd moved into the neighborhood, she'd had long, drabby blond hair.

We all said hello to her and she disappeared a moment, then came into the room with a tray of drinks in her hands. She was wearing a red, netlike dress which clung tightly to the curves of her plump body. When she bent over to put the tray down on the blondwood coffee table, the bosom of the dress slipped away from her tight, black brassière. I noticed Frank's pointed stare, then Elsie straightened up with a brassy, hostesslike smile and looked at Phil. Anne introduced them.

"Hel-*lo*," Elsie said. "I'm so glad you could come." She looked at us. "Well," she said, "name your poison."

What happened that evening up to the point when it all began is not important. There were the usual peregrinations to the kitchen and the bathroom; the usual breaking up and re-gathering of small groups—the women, the men, Frank, Phil and myself, Elizabeth and Anne, Elsie and Phil, Ron and me—and so on; the drifting knots of conversation that take place at any get-together.

There was record music and a little sporadic attempt at dancing. There was Candy stumbling into the living room, blinking and numb with only half-broken sleep; being tucked back into her bed. There were the expected personality displays—Frank, cynical and bored; Elizabeth, quietly radiant in her pregnancy; Phil, amusing and quick; Ron, mute and affable; Anne, soft-spoken and casual; Elsie, bouncing and strainedly vivacious.

One bit of conversation I remember: I was just about to go next door to check on Richard when Elsie said something about our getting a baby-sitter.

"It doesn't matter when you just go next door like this," she said, "but you do have to get out once in a while." Once in a while, to Elsie, meant an average of four nights a week.

"We'd like to," Anne said, "but we just haven't been able to find one."

"Try ours," said Elsie. "She's a nice kid and real reliable."

That was when I left and checked on Richard—and had one of my many nighttime adorations; that standing in semi-darkness over your child's crib and staring down at him. Nothing else. Just standing there and staring down at his little sleep-flushed face and feeling that almost overwhelming rush of absolute love in yourself. Sensing something close to holy in the same little being that nearly drove you out of your mind that very afternoon.

I turned up the heat a little then and went back to Elsie's house.

They were talking about hypnotism. I say *they* but, outside of Phil, Anne and maybe Frank, no one there knew the least thing about it. Primarily, it was a dissertation by Phil on one of his favorite topics.

"Oh, I don't believe that," Elsie said as I sat down beside Anne and whispered that Richard was fine. "People who say they were hypnotized weren't, really."

"Of course they were," Phil said. "If they weren't, how could they have hatpins jabbed into their throats without bleeding? Without even crying out?"

Elsie turned her head halfway to the side and looked at Phil in that overdone, accusingly dubious way that people affect when they have to bolster their own uncertain doubts.

"Did you ever *really* see anyone get a hatpin jabbed in their throat?" she said.

"I've had a five-inch hatpin in *my* throat," Phil answered. "And, once, I put one halfway through a friend of mine's arm at school—after I'd hypnotized him."

Elsie shuddered histrionically. *"Uhh,"* she said, "how *awful.*"

"Not at all," Phil said with that casual tone undergraduates love to affect when they are flicking off intellectual bomb-shells. "I didn't feel a thing and neither did my friend."

"Oh, you're just making that up," Elsie said, studiedly disbelieving.

"Not at all," said Phil.

It was Frank who gave it the final, toppling push.

"All right," he said, "let's see you hypnotize somebody then." He squeezed out one of his faintly cruel smiles. "Hypnotize Elsie," he said.

"Oh, no you don't!" Elsie squealed. "I'm not going to do terrible things in front of everybody."

"I thought you didn't believe in it," Phil said, amusedly.

"I don't, I don't," she insisted. "But . . . well, not *me.*"

Frank's dark eyes moved. "All right," he said, "who's going to be hypnotized?"

"I wouldn't suggest me unless we want to spend the whole night here," Anne said. "Phil used to waste hours trying to hypnotize me."

"You're a lousy subject, that's all," Phil said, grinning at her.

"Okay, who's it gonna be then?" Frank persisted. "How about you, Lizzie?"

"Oh . . ." Elizabeth lowered her eyes and smiled embarrassedly.

"We promise not to make you take your clothes off," Frank said.

*"Frank."* Elizabeth was thirty-one but she still blushed like a little girl. She wouldn't look at anybody. Elsie giggled. Frank looked only vaguely pleased. Elizabeth was too easy a mark for him.

"Come on, Elsie," he said, "be a sport. Let him put you under. We won't make you do a strip tease on the kitchen table."

"You—" Ron started to say.

"Oh, you're awful!" Elsie said, delighted.

"What were you going to say, Ron?" I asked.

Ron swallowed. "I—I was going to ask Phil," he said, "you—can't make someone—do what they don't want to do, can you? I mean—what they *wouldn't* do? If they were awake, I mean."

"Oh, what do *you* know about hypnotism, Ronny?"

Elsie asked, trying to sound pleasantly amused. The acidity still came through.

"Well, it's true and it isn't true," Phil said. "You can't make a subject break his own moral code. *But*—you can make almost any act fit into his moral code."

"How do you mean?" Frank asked. "This sounds promising."

"Well, for instance," Phil said, "if I hypnotized your wife—"

"You could make her do something *wicked*?" Frank asked, looking at Elizabeth pointedly.

"Frank, please," she almost whispered.

"Say I put a loaded gun in her hand," Phil said, "and told her to shoot you. She wouldn't do it."

"That's what you think," Frank said, snickering. I looked at Elizabeth again and saw her swallowing dryly. She was one of those pale and pitiable creatures who seem constantly vulnerable to hurt. You want to protect them and yet you can't. Of course Frank wasn't the easiest man in the world to live with either.

"Well, for argument's sake," Phil said, smiling a little, "we'll assume she wouldn't shoot you."

"Okay, for argument's sake," Frank said. He glanced at Elizabeth, a hint of that cruel smile on his lips again.

"*But*," Phil said, "if I were to tell Elizabeth that you were going to strangle her and told her that the only defense in the world she had was to shoot you right away—well, she might very well shoot you."

"How true," said Frank.

"Oh, I don't believe that," said Elsie.

"That's right," I joined in. "We have a friend named Alan Porter—he's a psychiatrist—and he gave a demonstration of that very thing. He had a young mother under hypnosis and he told her he was going to kill her baby and the only way she could stop him was by stabbing him with the knife she was holding—

it was a piece of cardboard. She stabbed him all right."

"Well, that's different," said Elsie. "Anyway, she was probably just playing along with a gag."

"Look," said Phil, gesturing dramatically with his hands, "I'll prove it to you right now if you want. Just let me hypnotize you."

"No, *sir*," said Elsie, "not me."

"How about you?" Phil asked Ron.

Ron mumbled something and shook his head with a faint smile. "He's already half hypnotized," said Elsie, kindly.

"Can't I get me a customer?" asked Phil. He sounded disappointed.

"How about you, Frank?" I asked.

"Uh-uh," he said, smiling as he blew out cigarette smoke. "Don't want ol' Lizzie knowing what's in my dirty old subconscious."

Elsie giggled and Elizabeth pressed her lips together, having failed in the attempt to smile.

"Well, that leaves you, brother man," said Phil, looking at me.

"You don't really think you could hypnotize *me*, do you?" I needled.

"Don't be so darn sure," he said, wagging a finger at me. "You arrogant ones are the first to topple."

I grinned, shrugging. "So what have I got to lose?" I said.

# TWO

FIRST OF ALL, PHIL ASKED THAT ALL THE lights be put out except for one dim wall lamp over the fireplace. Then he had me stretch out on the sofa while Ron went into the kitchen to get extra chairs. Gradually, everyone settled down. When the rustlings, comments and coughs had finally ceased, Phil spoke.

"Now I can't promise anything," he said.

"You mean we're going through all this for nothing?" Elsie asked.

"Some people are harder to hypnotize than others, that's all," Phil said. "I don't know about Tom. But you, for instance, Elsie, would be a good subject, I'm sure."

"Flattery will get you nowhere," Elsie said. "You just hypnotize your brother-in-law."

Phil turned back to me.

"All right, brother man, you ready?" he asked.

"Yes, sir, Mr. Cagliostro."

Phil pointed at me. "You just watch out," he said, "I have a feeling you're going to be a good subject."

"That's me," I said.

"Okay." Phil shifted in his chair. "Now everybody get quiet, please. Any distraction will break it up until the actual hypnosis takes place." He leaned forward and held out his forefinger again.

"Look at it," he said to me.

"Fine looking finger," I said. Frank snickered.

"Quiet, please," Phil said. He held the finger about six inches from my eyes. "Look at it," he said. "Keep looking at it. Don't look at anything else, just my finger."

"Why, what's it gonna do?" I asked.

"Poke you right in the eye if you don't *fermez* your big fat *bouche*." Phil jabbed the finger at me and I shut my eyes instinctively.

"All right," Phil said, "open 'em up. Let's try again."

"Yes, *sir*," I said.

"Now look at the finger. Just the finger. Don't look at anything else. Keep looking at the finger, the finger. I don't want you to look at anything but the finger."

"Your nail is dirty," I said.

Everybody laughed. Phil sank back in his chair with a grimace and pressed his thumb and forefinger to his eyes.

"Like I said," he said, "a lousy subject."

He looked over at Elsie.

"How about it?" he said. "I'm sure I could hypnotize you."

"Uh-uh." Elsie shook her close-cropped head vigorously.

"Let him try, Elsie," Ron said.

*"No-o."* Elsie glared at him as if he'd suggested something vile.

"Come on, champ," I said to Phil, "let's put me under now."

"You gonna play it straight," he asked, "or you gonna play it for the gallery?"

"I'll be good, sir, Mr. Mesmer, sir."

"You will like . . ." Phil leaned forward again, then settled back. "Well, let's forget the finger," he said. "Close your eyes."

"Close my eyes," I said. I did.

"Dark, isn't it?" said Frank.

I opened my eyes. "Not now," I said.

"Will you close your eyes, you clunk," Phil said. I did. I took a deep breath and settled back on the pillow. I could hear the slight breathings and chair-creakings of the others.

"All right," said Phil, "I want you to listen to me now."

I pretended to snore. I heard Elsie's explosive giggle; then I opened my eyes and looked at Phil's disgusted face.

"All right, all right," I promised, "I'll be good." I closed my eyes. "Go ahead," I said, "I'll be good."

"Honest *Indian?*" Phil enunciated.

"That's pretty strong language to use in the company of these fine women," I said. "However, honest, as you say, Indian."

"All right. Shut your eyes then, you bum."

"Now that's a poor way to win my confidence," I said. "How am I supposed to venerate you when you talk to me like that? Alan Porter doesn't—"

"Will you shut your fat eyes?" Phil interrupted.

"Shut. Shut," I said. "You may fire when griddy, Redley."

Phil took a deep and weary breath. "Oh, well," he said. Then he started talking again.

"I want you to pretend you're in a theatre," he

said. "An enormous theatre. You're sitting near the front. It's completely black inside."

Across the room I heard Elizabeth's slight, apologetic throat-clearing.

"There's no light in the theatre," Phil went on. "It's completely dark—like black velvet. The walls are covered with black velvet. The seats are all made of black velvet."

"Expensive," I said.

They all laughed. "Oh . . . *shoot,*" Phil said. I opened my eyes and grinned at him.

"I'm sorry, I'm sorry," I said.

"Oh . . . the heck you are."

"Yes, I am. I am." I closed my eyes tight. "See? See? I'm back in the theatre again. I'm in the loges. What's playing?"

"You are a son of a b," said Phil.

"Sir," I said, "control. Go ahead. If I don't stay quiet, I give you permission to hit me on the head."

"Don't think I won't," Phil said. "Someone hand me that lamp." He was quiet a moment. Then he said, "You really want to go on with it?"

"Brother *man,*" I said.

"*You* . . ." Phil cleared his throat. "All right," he said, patiently.

I won't go into the complete progression; it took too long. It's hard to get serious when you're in a group like that. Especially when Phil and I were so used to heckling each other. I'm afraid I broke up many a moment when he thought he had me. After a while Elsie got bored and went in the kitchen to get food ready. Frank began to talk softly with Anne and direct an occasional, acidulous comment our way. A good hour must have passed and we were still nowhere. I don't know why Phil kept on. He must have felt I was a challenge. At any rate, he wouldn't give up. He kept on with that theatre bit and, after a while,

Frank stopped talking and watched and, except for a slight clinking of dishes in the kitchen, there was only the monotonous sound of Phil's voice, talking at me.

"The walls are dark velvet, the floors are covered with dark velvet rugs. It's black inside, absolutely black. Except for one thing. In the whole pitch-black theatre there's only one thing you can see. The letters up on the screen. Tall, thin, white letters on the black, black screen. They spell *sleep*. Sleep. You're very comfortable, very comfortable. You're just sitting there and looking at the screen, looking, looking at that single word up there. Sleep. Sleep. Sleep."

I'll never know what made it begin to work on me unless it was sheer repetition. I suspect my assurance that I couldn't be hypnotized helped too; an assurance of such illogical magnitude that I took it for granted. I didn't even *try* to get hypnotized. To quote Elsie— I just played along with the gag.

"You're relaxing," Phil said. "Your feet and ankles are relaxed. Your legs are relaxed, so relaxed. Your hands are limp and heavy. Your arms are relaxed, so relaxed. You're beginning to relax all over. Relax. Relax. You're going to sleep. To sleep. You're going to sleep."

And I was. I started slipping away. By the time I felt the slightest trickle of awareness as to what was happening to me, it was too late. It was as if my mind—or, rather, my volition—were a moth being set into congealing wax. There was a faint fluttering as I tried to escape; but all in vain. I began to feel as I had once when I had an impacted wisdom tooth taken out. The oral surgeon had jabbed a needle into the exposed vein on my left arm. I'd asked him what it was for and he'd said it was to stop excess salivation. I guess that's what they always say so the patient won't be afraid. Because it wasn't for that, it was a fast-acting general anesthetic. The room started weaving around me, everything got watery in front of me, the nurses leaning over me wavered as if I were looking at them through lenses of jelly. And then I woke up; it was that fast. I didn't even realize when I'd lost consciousness. It seemed as if I'd closed my eyes only a second or two. I'd been out cold for forty-five minutes.

It was just like that again. I opened my eyes and saw Phil sitting there grinning at me. I blinked at him.

"What'd I do, doze off?" I asked.

Phil chuckled. I looked around. They were all looking at me in different ways; Frank, curious; Ron, baffled; Elizabeth blank; Elsie half afraid. Anne looked concerned.

"Are you all right, honey?" she asked me.

"Sure. Why?" I looked at her a moment. Then I sat up. "You don't mean to tell me it took?" I said, incredulously.

"Did it ever," she said, her smile only half amused.

"I was hypnotized?"

That seemed to break the tension. Everybody seemed to talk at once.

"I'll be damned," said Frank.

"My goodness," said Elizabeth. Ron shook his head wonderingly.

"Were you really *hypnotized?*" Elsie asked. There was very little distrust left in her voice.

"I . . . guess I was," I said.

"You know it," Phil said, unable to stop grinning.

I looked at Anne again. "I really was?" I asked.

"If you weren't, you're the best little actor I ever saw," she said.

"I never saw anything like it," Ron said quietly.

"How do you feel?" Phil asked me and I knew, from the way he said it, it was a loaded question.

"How should I feel?" I asked, suspiciously.

Phil forced down his grin. "A little . . . hot?" he asked.

Suddenly, I realized that I *was* hot. I ran my hand over my forehead and rubbed away sweat. I felt as if I'd been sitting in the sun too long.

"What did you do—set fire to me?" I asked.

Phil laughed out loud. "We tried," he said, "but you wouldn't catch."

Then he calmly told me that, while I was stretched out like a board between two kitchen chairs, he'd sat on my stomach and run a cigarette-lighter flame back and forth along my exposed legs.

I just sat there gaping at him.

"Let's have that again," I said.

"That's right," he said, laughing, delighted at his success. I looked over at Anne again.

"This happened?" I asked, weakly. She got up, smiling, and came over to me. Sitting down she put her arm around me.

"You sure are a dandy subject, love," she said. Her voice shook a little when she said it.

Ten minutes later we were all sitting around the kitchen table, discussing my hypnotism. I must say it was the first time I'd ever heard an animated discussion in Elsie's house.

"I didn't," I said, laughing.

"You sure did." Anne made an amused sound. "There you were, twelve years old again, telling us about somebody named Joey Ariola—who must have been a beast from the way you talked about him."

"Ariola." I shook my head wonderingly. "I'll be damned. I'd forgotten all about him."

"You just thought you'd forgotten," Phil said.

"Oh . . . I don't believe anybody can remember that far back," Elsie said. "He was just making it up or something."

"He could go back a lot farther than that," Phil told her. "There are authenticated cases where subjects go back to prenatal days."

"To what?"

"To before they were born."

"Oh . . ." Elsie turned her head halfway to the side again. Now that the vision of me stretched calcified between two of her kitchen chairs was beginning to fade, she was regaining dissent.

"That's right," Phil said. "And there's Bridey Murphy."

"Who?" asked Elsie.

"A woman who, under hypnosis, claims she was an Irish girl in her previous life."

"Oh . . . that's silly," Elsie said. Everybody was quiet for a moment and Elsie looked up at the clock. She shrugged at Phil.

"It's not time yet," Phil said.

"Time for what?" I asked.

"You'll see," Phil told me.

Elsie got up and went over to the stove. "Who wants more coffee?" she asked. I looked at Phil a moment longer, then let it go.

"What else did I say when I was—I mean when I thought I was twelve again?" I asked Anne.

She smiled and shook her head. "Oh . . . all sorts of things," she said. "About your father and—your mother. About a bike you wanted that had a foxtail on the handlebars."

"Oh, my God, yes," I said, delighted at the sudden recollection. "I remember that. Lord, how I wanted that bike."

"I wanted something else when I was twelve," said Frank.

I noticed how Elizabeth looked down at her coffee, her pale red lips pressed together. Everything about Elizabeth was pale; the shade of her lipstick, the blond of her hair, the color of her skin. She seemed, in a way, to be partially vanished.

"I wasn't after any bike at twelve," Frank said.

"Man, we know what you were after," I said, trying to make it sound like the joke that Frank had not intended it to be. "What else did I talk about?" I asked Anne before Frank could say any more.

I noticed Ron looking up at the clock now, then glancing over at Phil. Phil pressed down a grin—as did Frank. Elsie came back to the table and put down another plate of little glazed cakes.

"Well, I don't think it's going to happen," she said. "It's already eleven."

"What's that?" I asked.

"Let's see," Anne said as if I hadn't spoken, "you talked about your sister and—about your room. About your dog."

For a second I remembered Corky and the way he had of putting his old shaggy head on my knees and staring at me.

"What's the joke?" I asked, because there was one obviously. "Why are you all looking like cats who swallowed the mice?"

At which point I took off my left shoe and put it into the refrigerator.

I turned to face their explosion of laughter. For a moment I actually didn't know what they were laughing about. Then, suddenly, I realized what I'd just done. I opened the refrigerator and peered in at my dark shoe placed neatly beside a covered bowl of peas.

"What'd you do that for?" Phil asked, innocently.

"I don't know," I said. "I—just wanted to, I guess. Why shouldn't—?" I stopped abruptly and looked at Phil accusingly. "You crumb, you," I said, "you gave me a post-hypnotic command."

Phil grinned, returned to glory again.

"He told you," Elsie declared. "You knew just what you were doing."

"No, I didn't," I said.

"You did so," said Elsie, pettishly.

"Say," said Frank, "what if Tom was a girl and you gave her the post-hypnotic command to—oh, well, never mind, my wife doesn't like that kind of talk. Do you, Lizzie old girl?"

"He's always making fun of me," she answered with attempted lightness. Her smile was pale too.

"I hope you didn't give me any other post-hypnotic suggestions, you idiot," I said.

Phil shook his head with a smile.

"Nope," he said, "that's all, brother man. It's over."

Famous last words.

# THREE

THE PARTY BROKE UP ABOUT ONE. Until then we sat around the kitchen table drinking coffee and putting down Elsie's high-calorie cakes; talking about what had happened during the hypnosis.

Apparently it had been a roaring success. I'd not only gone rigid between those chairs, I'd laughed like a crazy man over nothing. I'd cried like a baby over nothing. That is, over nothing visible. Of course I had something to laugh and cry over. Phil was feeding it to me.

And I shivered and chattered my teeth on an ice floe in the Arctic. I sweated and gasped for water as I lay on the blazing sands of the Sahara. I drank too much nonexistent whiskey—glass by glass—and got owl-eyed, silly drunk. I grew knotted up with fury, my face hard and red, my body shuddering with repressed hatred. I listened to a Rachmaninoff piano concerto played by Rachmaninoff himself and told everyone how beautiful, how magnificent it sounded. I held out my arm and Frank hung from it and Phil stuck straight pins into it.

A roaring success.

I guess we could have gone on all night talking about it. It isn't every day that such intriguing fare enters one's life. But we had two expectant mothers on our hands and they needed their rest. Besides which, I suspected Elsie got a little fed up after a while. It was too far removed from her scope to be more than passingly interesting.

Anne, Phil and I said good night to Frank and Elizabeth after we'd left Elsie's house and they went across Tulley Street to their house as we went to ours.

There was a half hour or so of mute-voiced preparation for bed. I got the army cot out of the closet in Richard's room and unfolded it while Anne got bedding from the hall closet. Phil made up the cot and then we all got into our pajamas, washed our faces, brushed our teeth, said our good-night words and retired.

I couldn't sleep.

I lay beside Anne, staring at the ceiling. There were springs in my eyes. If I shut them they jumped open again. I kept staring at the ceiling and listening to the sounds of the night—the rustle of a breeze-stirred bush outside the window, the creak of the mattress as Anne moved a little, the faint crackling settle of the house; up the street, a dog barking briefly at some imagined foe, then relapsing into sleep.

I swallowed dryly and sighed. I turned on my side and stared at the dark bulk of the bureau.

"What's the matter?" Anne asked, softly.

"Oh . . . can't sleep," I answered.

"You sick?"

"No. Too much coffee, I guess."

"Oh. You shouldn't drink it at night."

"I know. Well . . . you go to sleep, sweetheart. I'll be all right."

"Okay." She sighed drowsily. "If you feel sick, wake me up, now," she said.

"I'm not sick." I leaned over and kissed her warm cheek. "Good night, little mother."

"Night."

She stretched out and I felt the warmth of her hip against mine. Then she was still except for the even sound of her breathing.

I lay there; waiting for something, it seemed. I just couldn't shut my eyes. I felt as I had at college after I'd spent about five hours at intense studying—my mind swimming with information and intelligences; turning over and over like a machine somebody forgot to turn off.

I rolled onto my side. Nothing. I turned on my back and closed my eyes. Sleep, I told myself. I had to grin in the darkness as I remembered Phil's earnest voice telling me to sleep, sleep. Well, by God, he'd succeeded. I couldn't needle him on that count. He'd really pulled a fast one. I would have laid odds he couldn't hypnotize me. But he did—and with not too much trouble either. As soon as I'd stopped razzing him and relaxed, it had happened.

I turned irritably onto my side again and punched at the pillow. I heard Anne mumble something and I clenched my teeth. I was going to wake her up again if I didn't stop this twisting and turning.

Why was I so restless? I'd had coffee, yes, but not a pot of it; maybe three cups altogether.

I frowned to myself. Was it possible the hypnosis had done this? Maybe Phil had forgotten to tie up loose mental ends. Maybe he'd given my brain a spin and neglected to break it.

No, that was ridiculous. He'd obviously known what he was doing. It was coffee and conversation. Living in this neighborhood I was taking too much of the first and getting too little of the second.

I sighed heavily. My brain was alive. That's the only way I can express it. Thoughts spun through it like heated gases, sparking and iridescent. Memories came and went like flashes of half-seen light. My mother, my father, Corky, high school, grammar school, nursery, college, campus grass, books I'd read, girls I'd loved, ham and eggs—exactly how they tasted.

I sat up and actually shook my head as one would shake a clock. Only I didn't want to start it, I wanted to stop it. But I couldn't. It seemed as if my mind were throbbing; like a living sponge in my head, swelling with hot juices of thought, squeezed of remembrance and devising.

I stood up, breathing harshly. My body was tingling, my chest and stomach felt taut. I moved across the rug, then stopped in the doorway and shut my eyes.

"My . . . *God*," I remember muttering, only half conscious of speaking. I shook my head. Thoughts were stampeding. Frank, Elizabeth, Ron, Elsie, Anne, Phil, my mother, my father; all of them running across the screen of my mind as if projected by some maniac cameraman. Dozens of half-shaped impressions zeroing in on me, knitting plastically into a hot core of multiformed awareness.

I swallowed again and went into the bathroom. I blinked at the glaring light, shut the door and stepped over to the mirror with a lurching movement. I stared at my blank face. It told me nothing.

*Something wrong.* I don't know whether I said or thought it. But the idea was there. Something *was* wrong. This was more than coffee nerves, more than animated talk rebounding. What it was, though, I didn't know, I didn't know at all.

I started to run a glass of water but the sound of the splashing seemed unnaturally loud and I twisted off the faucet. I drank a little but it tasted like cold acid and I poured it out and set the glass down.

Turning, I flicked off the light, opened the door and padded to the doorway of Richard's room. I listened. All I could hear was Phil's breathing. I stepped over to the crib and put my palm on Richard's back. They're so quiet at night, I remember thinking distractedly. Then I felt the faint rise and fall of his back and I drew away my hand.

I went into the hall again, trying to calm myself. I walked into the living room and looked out the back window a while. I could see the dark shape of Richard's wagon out on the back-yard grass and, over on the next block, the bleak illumination of a street lamp. The neighborhood was deathly still.

I twisted around suddenly.

Nothing. Just darkness and the black outlines of the furniture. Yet I would have sworn I'd heard something. I shuddered and felt the muscles of my stomach draw in spastically. I ran a shaking hand through my hair. What in God's name was happening?

I walked to the other side of the room and sank down on an easy chair. I sighed and lay my head back wearily. The tingling at my temples increased. I could almost feel it physically. I put my fingers to my temples but there was nothing. I put my hands on my lap and stretched out my legs.

*Rising.* Something was rising in me. As if I were a vessel into which was being poured alien cognizance. I felt things, sensed things—things I couldn't understand, things I couldn't even clearly see; shards of strange perception. Perceptions impossible to grasp— flowings and flashings in my mind. It was like standing on a fogbound corner and seeing unknown people rushing by—close enough to catch a glimpse of, not close enough to recognize. It got stronger and stronger. Awareness deluged into my mind. I was the channel for a million images.

Which stopped. I raised my head.

Until that moment I had never known what it was to be so afraid my breath was stopped, my body functionless, myself incapable of doing anything but stare in helpless shock.

She was in her thirties, pale, her hair in black disarray. She was wearing a strange, dark dress with a single strand of pearls at her throat. I sat rooted to the chair, my limbs dead. I stared at her.

I don't know how many minutes passed while that woman and I looked at each other. It didn't occur to me to wonder why it was I could see her so clearly in the darkness, why there was a sort of sourceless light on or rather, *in* her.

Minutes passed. I knew that something had to break the awful silence. I opened my mouth to speak but couldn't. There was a dry, clicking sound in my throat.

Then, abruptly, breath spilled from my lips.

*"Who are you?"* I gasped.

The woman edged back—although I never saw her limbs move. She was almost to the window.

And breath was gone again—gone with a sucking sound of terror. I felt myself pressing back against the chair, my eyes stiffly set, my lips shaking. Because I could see the lamp on the next street—

*through her.*

My cry was weak and short—a strangling sound in my throat. I sat there looking at the spot where the woman had been standing. How long I sat there I don't know. I couldn't get up. I must have been there for an hour or more before I dared to stand and slowly, tremblingly, as if I were stalking something deadly, move over to the spot where she had been.

Nothing.

I turned and rushed into the bedroom. It was only when I had slid frightenedly under the covers that I realized how cold I was. I started to shiver and couldn't stop for a long time. Fortunately, Anne was sleeping soundly. At least five times I started to wake her up to tell her—but every time I was stopped by the thought of how frightened she would be. Finally, I decided to tell her in the morning. I even tried to tell myself I'd had a nightmare, that it really hadn't happened at all.

Unfortunately, I knew better. I knew that something had happened to me that I'd never believed could happen to anyone. So simple to put the word itself down; all it takes is a few elementary turns of the pencil. Yet it can change your entire life.

The word is *ghost*.

# FOUR

**I** SPOKE IT THE NEXT MORNING AT BREAK-
fast.

I'd been unable to when we'd first gotten up. For
a few minutes, of course, there was the inevitable rush
of rejection toward what I'd seen. What I'd tried to
do the night before, I tried again—to believe that it
was only a febrile dream. One's mind can far more
easily accept that sort of explanation. There's reason
to it, something to grasp hold of; even when it isn't
true.

I'd been unable to speak, too, because it seemed so
completely inappropriate. It just didn't fit in with good
mornings and kissings and dressing and getting Sunday breakfast ready.

But when Richard was finished eating and had
gone out into the yard to play, and Anne and Phil
and I were sitting at the kitchen table over coffee, I
did say it.

"I saw a ghost last night."

It's fantastic how the most terrifying of statements can sound absurd. Phil's reaction was to grin. Even Anne smiled a little.

"You what?" she asked.

Her smile was the first to fade. It went as soon as she saw how serious I was.

"Honey, what do you mean?" she asked. "You dreamed it?"

I swallowed. It's not what one could call the easiest thing in the world to talk about.

"I'd like to think that," I said, "but I . . . can't." I looked at them both. "I really saw one. I mean I was awake and I *saw* one."

"This is on the level?" Phil asked.

I didn't say anything. I just nodded.

"When?" Anne asked.

I put down my cup.

"After I got up last night," I said. "That is, this morning. It must have been about two."

"I didn't hear you get up," she said.

"You were asleep," I told her. Even as I spoke, a rush of crude hope filled me that it really had been a dream.

"This was—after you told me you couldn't sleep?" she asked. I could tell she didn't believe me; rather, didn't believe that I'd seen what I said I'd seen.

I said yes. I looked at both of them and shrugged with a helpless, palms-up gesture. "That's it," I said. "I saw a ghost. I saw it."

"What did it look like?" Phil asked. He didn't even try to conceal his fascination. This was meat for him.

I drew in a ragged breath, then shrugged again as if I felt slightly ashamed of what I was saying. As a matter of fact I think I was; a little.

"It was a woman," I said. "She was—in her thirties, I'd say. Had dark hair and—was about, oh, five-foot-six. She was wearing an odd dress—black with a strange design on it. And there was a string of pearls around her neck."

There was a moment's suspension, then Anne said, "You *saw* this?"

"I saw it," I said. "I was in the living room, sitting on the green chair. I looked up and—she was standing there." I swallowed. "Looking at me."

"Honey . . ." I couldn't tell what I heard more of in her voice—sympathy or revulsion.

"You really saw it then," said Phil, "I mean with your eyes?"

"Phil, I told you," I said, "I *saw* it. It wasn't a dream. Let's toss that out right now. It *happened*. I got up, I went into the bathroom. I heard you sleeping. I checked Richard to see if he was all right, I looked out the back window at the yard. I sat down on the green chair—and I saw her. Like that. I was awake. It wasn't any dream."

I noticed how Anne was looking at me. It was a complex look, compounded of many things—curiosity, withdrawal, concern, love, fear; all of them in the one look.

"Before this happened," Phil said, "what was your mental state? I mean, why couldn't you sleep?"

I looked at him curiously. "Why?" I asked.

"Because I think you were in a state of mental turmoil. Before you—let's say—saw what you did."

"Phil, I *did* see it," I said, a little impatiently now. "Come on. I just won't go along with this dream idea. Don't, for God's sake, humor me. I'm not a mental case."

"Of course you're not," Phil said quickly. "I didn't mean that for a second. What you saw was as real to you as I am, sitting here across from you."

I didn't know exactly what he was driving at but I said, "Okay, then. That's settled."

"You *were* in an aroused mental state, though," Phil said. It wasn't a question this time.

I looked at him a moment, warily. I didn't want to be led to any pat conclusion about this. But of course I had to say yes to his statement.

"All right," he said, "and I imagine you even have a headache now. Do you?"

"A little one." I felt myself start. "How do you know all this?" I asked.

"Because it follows a pattern, brother man," he said. "You had a hallucination as a result of—"

"Phil . . ." I started.

"Listen to me."

"Phil, it wasn't a hallucination! You were right before, not now. What I saw was as real to me as you are, sitting there."

"Of course it was. Do you think that makes it actual?"

That stopped me cold. It's the sort of question that can topple anything; make even the most objective reality spin away into tenuous nothingness. I sat there staring at him blankly, feeling that light pulse of pain in my head.

"What do you mean?" I finally asked.

"Simply this," he said, "people have had hallucinations before—in broad daylight, much less dead of night. They've shaken hands with their hallucinations, talked with them."

"What you're trying to say," I said, unable to keep from smiling a little, "is that your old brother-in-law is ready for the hatch."

"Oh, hell, no," Phil said. "That woman exists. I don't know where—or when. But she's real. I mean she lives somewhere—or did live somewhere. She's someone you've known or seen—or maybe haven't seen; that isn't necessary. The point is, what you saw wasn't a ghost. Not in the usual sense of the word anyway—though plenty of so-called ghosts would fit into this category."

"Which is?" I asked.

"Telepathic images," Phil said. "If one person can see a card with a symbol on it, another person can see what looks like a human being. I mean *see* it. Your mind was keyed up high because of our little experiment last night. You saw this woman. Naturally, the first thing you thought of was ghost. That's the trouble with our attitude—not just yours, Tom.

"People won't believe in reasonable, verifiable phenomena—things like hypnotism, telepathy, clairvoyance. No, that they won't accept. But they *see* something and, in a second—whammo!—they're off the edge, flying high. Because they're not prepared, because they can only react with instinctive emotion. They won't accept reasonable things with their minds but the fantastic things they'll swallow whole when their emotions are brought into play. Because the emotions have no limits on belief. The emotions will swallow anything—and they do. As witness yourself. You're an intelligent man, Tom. But the only thing you thought of was ghost."

He paused and Anne and I stared at him. He'd sounded just like Alan Porter.

"*The* end," he said, grinning. "Pass the basket."

"So you don't think I saw it then," I said.

"You *did* see it," he answered, "but in your mind's eye. And, believe me, brother man, seeing it that way can be just as realistic to you as seeing it the ordinary way. Sometimes a lot more realistic."

He grinned. "Hell, man," he said, "you were a medium last night."

We talked about it some more. I didn't have much to offer, though—except objections. It's a little hard to let go of a thing like that. Maybe the human reaction is to cling to it a little. As Phil had indicated, it's a lot more "romantic" to see a ghost. Not so really thrilling to write it off as "mere" telepathy.

It was Anne who broke it up.

"Well, we're doing a lot of talking about this," she said with her true woman's mind, "but we're missing the whole point. What I want to know is—who *was* this woman?"

Phil and I both had to laugh at the combination of curiosity and wifely suspicion in her voice.

"Who else?" Phil said. "One of his girl friends."

I shook my head.

"I wish I knew," I said, "but I can't remember ever seeing her." I shrugged. "Maybe it was—what's her name?—Helen Driscoll."

"Whoozat, whoozat?" Phil asked.

"She's the woman who used to live in this house," Anne told him. "She's Mrs. Sentas' sister; the woman who lives next door."

"Oh." Phil shrugged. "Could be."

"So I saw the ghost of Helen Driscoll," I said, straight-faced.

"Except for one little thing," Anne said.

"What?" Phil asked.

"She's not dead. She just went back east."

"Not west," said Phil.


The headache got worse. So much worse that I had to beg off going to the beach that afternoon. I made them go without me; told Anne not to worry, I'd take an aspirin and lie down until the headache went away.

They went a few minutes past two, piling into Phil's coupe with basket, blanket, beach bag, lotions, et al. I stood on the porch waving to Richard as the Mercury gunned up Tulley Street. Like so many young men Phil liked to be doing about fifty before he shifted into third.

I watched until the car turned left onto the boulevard; then I went back inside the house. As I started to close the door I saw Elizabeth out on her lawn again, white-gloved, poking a trowel at the garden soil. She had on a wide-brimmed straw hat that she and Frank had bought in Tijuana. She didn't look over at me. I stood there a moment watching her slow, tired movements. The term "professional martyr" occurred to me and I put it off as unworthy.

I shut the sight of her away with the door. Anyway, I had my own troubles. For a moment I wondered where Frank was, deciding that he was either sleeping in his house or else stretched out on the beach, ogling girls. I shook that off too. It simply wasn't my business.

I turned and stood looking at the spot where the woman had been. A shudder plaited down my back. I tried to visualize her but it was hard in the daylight. I went over to the exact spot and stood on it, feeling the warmth of the sunlight on my ankles. It was almost impossible to believe that it hadn't been a dream.

I went into the kitchen and put on some water for coffee. I leaned against the edge of the sink counter while I waited for it to boil. It was very quiet in the house. I stared down at the multicolored spatter design on the linoleum until it swam before my eyes. In the cupboard I could hear the alarm clock ticking. It reminded me of Poe's story about the telltale heart. It *sounded* like a heart beating hollowly behind the shielding of the cabinet door. I closed my eyes and sighed. Why couldn't I believe Phil? Everything he'd said had been so sensible—on the surface.

There was my answer, I decided. What I felt wasn't on the surface. It was a subterranean trickle of awareness far beneath the level of consciousness. All right, it was emotion. Perhaps emotion was a better gauge for things like that.

"I said come *in* here!"

I started with a gasp, my head jerking up so fast it sent electric twinges along my neck muscles. For a moment, I actually expected to see the woman in the strange black dress standing before me again.

"Ron!" I heard then. "I mean *now!*"

I swallowed and blew out a long, trembling breath.

"All right," I heard. "*All* right. What about *that?*"

I couldn't hear Ron's answer. You never could. Elsie might have been conducting a vituperative monologue across the alley.

"I told you at breakfast, damn it, *I don't want your damn clothes laying all over my house!*"

Amusement broke into sound in my throat and I shook my head slowly. Dear God, I thought; *her* house. She didn't want his clothes lying all over her house. Ron was a boarder there, not the legal owner. A man's home is his castle, I thought, unless his wife makes him live in the dungeon. I wondered for a diverting moment what kind of match Ron and Elizabeth would make. One thing for sure, I decided, it would be the quietest damn house on the block.

"And what about the oven?" Elsie asked. "You said you were going to clean it this weekend. Well, *have* you?"

It made me cringe to hear talk like that. I felt my hands curling up into instinctive fists.

"One of these days," I muttered, half myself, half imagining myself as Ron, "one of these days. *Pow!* Right to the moon!"

My punch at the air sent jagged lines of pain through my head. Laughter faded with a wince. I couldn't stay amused anyway. There was my own problem. It wasn't over. No matter what Phil said, it wasn't over.

I was drinking my coffee when I heard bare feet

padding in the alley. I looked up and saw Elsie come up onto the back porch. Through the film of the door curtains, I saw that she was wearing a black bathing suit.

She knocked. "Anne?" she called.

I got up and opened the door.

"Oh, *hi*," she said, quickly rearranging her smile from one of polite neighborliness to one of mathematical seduction. At least that was the effect I got.

"Good afternoon," I said.

The bathing suit clung to her plumpness as if she'd been dipped into it rather than pulled it on.

"Tom, could I borrow those raffia-covered glasses?" she asked. "I'm having some relatives over tonight."

"Yeah. Sure." I backed away a step, then turned for the cupboard. I heard her come in the kitchen and shut the door.

"Where's Anne?" she asked. The sound of the question was innocent. Yet, for some reason, I knew it wasn't.

"Gone to the beach," I told her.

"You mean you're all alone?" she said. "Yum yum." It was supposed to be a joke but, like Frank, Elsie was incapable of obscuring her motive with words.

"That's right," I said, pulling open the cabinet door. Suddenly I felt that tingling in my temples again. It made my hand twitch. I looked back over my shoulder, half expecting to see that woman. There was only Elsie.

"You should have told me," she minced. "I'd have put on something more—appropriate."

I swallowed and took down the glasses. I had the very definite inclination to tell her to get out of the house. I didn't know why. There was just something about her that disturbed me. And it wasn't the obvious thing either.

"How long are they going to be gone?" Elsie asked.

I turned with the glasses.

"Why do you ask?" I made the mistake of smiling as I said it.

To Elsie it probably looked as if I slipped at that moment. I didn't. I reeled as a wave of raw sensation hit me. I caught for balance at the sink and managed to catch myself without breaking a glass.

"No reason," she said, obviously taking my slip for a form of fluster. "Why? Should I have?"

I stood there looking at her. She wasn't smiling. She stood there without moving, one hand on the outjutting curve of a hip. I noticed the line of dewy sweat across her upper lip and how the sunlight behind her was shining through the golden aura of hair along the edges of her shoulders, arms and neck.

"Guess not." I walked over and handed her the glasses. I don't know whether it was an accident that our hands touched. I jerked mine away a little too quickly to hide it.

"What's the matter, Tom?" she asked with the tone of voice used by a woman who is convinced she's irresistible.

"Nothing," I said.

"You're blushing!"

I knew I wasn't; and realized that it was a trick she used to fluster the men she flirted with.

"Am I?" I said coldly. That desire was thrusting itself through me; the desire to push her violently from the house.

"Yes," she said. "I'm not embarrassing you in this suit, am I?"

"Not at all," I said. I felt physically ill standing so close to her. She seemed to radiate something that wrenched my insides. I turned to the door and opened it. "I have a little headache, that's all," I explained. "I was just about to lie down."

*"Oh-h."* The sympathy was false too; I felt it. "You lie down then. Lying down can help a lot—of things." She finished as if it were an afterthought.

"Yes. I will."

"I'll bring the glasses back tonight," she said.

"No hurry," I answered. I wanted to scream into her face—*Will you get the hell out of here!* Repressing it made me shiver.

"That was quite a party we had last night," said Elsie. Her voice seemed to come from a distance. I couldn't see her face distinctly.

"Yes," I managed to say, "very interesting."

"You really knew what you were doing, though, didn't you?" she told me.

I nodded quickly, willing to say anything to get her out. "Yes. Of course."

"I *knew* it," she said, satisfied. I closed the door halfway. *"Well."* Elsie took a deep breath and the bathing suit swelled in front. "Thanks for the glasses," she said as if she were thanking me for something else.

I closed the door behind her and gasped dizzily.

*"Get in that back yard!"* Elsie screamed.

I jumped so sharply I banged my knee against the door. As I bent over, rubbing it, I heard Candy outside in the alley, whining.

When Elsie was gone I sank down at the table and closed my eyes. I felt as if I'd just climbed out of a well. I tried to tell myself it was only imagination but that didn't work. Mind ran second again, poor competition for my emotions. I felt dazed and weakened. On the surface that was senseless. Elsie was quite ordinary, not very attractive. She'd never bothered me before. I'd always felt slightly amused by her antics.

I wasn't amused now. I almost felt afraid of her.

And, no matter how I went about it, there was only one explanation. I'd seen behind her words, behind her actions. Somehow I'd been inside her mind.

It was an awful place.

# FIVE

I TOLD ANNE ABOUT IT THAT NIGHT AFTER Phil had left for Berkeley. Richard was asleep and we were getting ready for bed. I was in my pajamas, Anne undressing by the closet.

"I don't understand what you mean," she said when I'd finished.

I shook my head slowly. "I don't blame you," I said somberly. "I don't understand it either."

"Well . . . what is it?" she asked. "You say you felt repelled by her but—" She didn't finish; just stood there looking at me.

"That's it," I said, "I—I think I must have known what was going on in her mind. I don't mean her thoughts exactly; not words or sentences." I gestured helplessly. "What was behind her words I guess. What she felt."

"My God," Anne said. "You make her sound like a monster."

"Maybe we're all monsters underneath," I said.

I saw her shudder a little as she drew on her robe. She came over and sat down beside me. We were quiet for a moment.

"All right," she said, "forgetting about Elsie for the moment. Do you think this is a carry-over from last night? Like . . . seeing that woman?"

"I don't know what else it could be," I told her.

She bit her lower lip. "What could have happened?" she asked.

"I don't know," I said. "You saw it. Did I act—strange in any way while I was under hypnosis?"

She looked at me worriedly. "Not that I can remember," she said. "I've seen people hypnotized before. I've seen Phil hypnotize other people. They didn't act any different from the way you did."

I sighed. "I don't get it then."

"You should have told Phil," she said. "Maybe he could have done something."

"How?" I asked. "As far as he was concerned the hypnosis was everything he wanted it to be. He'd just say I'm a little keyed up."

"I know, but . . ."

She looked so disturbed that I tried to sound a little less worried about it.

"Telepathy, you can have it."

"You really think that's what it is?"

"I don't know what it is." I shrugged. "I guess that's as good a word as any."

"It's—such a remote word," she said. "You hear it spoken once in a blue moon. You read about it occasionally. But you never really think about it in personal terms."

"Well, maybe I'm just jumping to conclusions," I said. "It may just be a simple old nervous breakdown."

She put her hand over mine.

"Well, if this . . . sort of thing goes on," she said, "we'll go to Alan Porter." She smiled wryly. "Or something."

I smiled back. "Or something; maybe to an asylum."

"Honey, don't talk like that."

"I'm sorry." I put my arms around her and we pressed together.

"I got a friend in here needs a daddy," she murmured. "Not some character in a padded cell."

I kissed her. "Tell your friend," I said, "I accept his terms."

I saw her again. It was the same as it had been the first time; the strange dark dress, the string of pearls at her throat, the hair all uncombed, a frame of tangled blackness around her white face. She was standing in the same way by the back window, looking at me. This time I could see more because I wasn't incapacitated by shock. I could see that she had a look of pleading on her face. As if she were asking me for something.

"Who are you?" I asked again.

Then I woke up.

For a few moments, a surge of almost overwhelming relief flooded through me—and, with it, recognition. Phil was right, it hadn't been a ghost. It hadn't even been telepathy but only a dream. She wasn't real. I was safe. All these thoughts in the space of seconds.

And gone sooner. Because I felt that tingling in my head again, that cramping tension in my guts. That same twisting aggravation of the flesh that had driven me from my bed the night before. And I knew—as surely as anything I had ever known—that, if I got up and walked into the living room, she'd be there waiting for me.

I pushed my face into the pillow and lay there shuddering, fighting it. I wasn't going in there. I simply wasn't going in there!

Suddenly I froze, listening. There was something in the hall; I heard the sound of it. A swishing crackle of a sound—*like the skirt of a moving woman.*

Abruptly, there was a cry.

*Richard!* A blade of terror plunged into my heart. Gasping, I threw back the covers and jumped up, rushed across the floor, lunging into the hall, into Richard's room. He was standing in his crib, crying and shivering in the darkness. Quickly, I pulled him up and pressed my cheek to his.

"Shhh, baby, it's all right," I whispered. "It's all right, daddy's here." I felt a shudder ripple down my back and I held him tightly, patting his back with shaking fingers. "It's all right baby; daddy's here. Go to sleep, sweetheart. It's all right."

I felt his fear; felt it as distinctly as if it were a current of icy water trickling from his brain to mine. "It's all right," I said. "Go to sleep now. Daddy's here." I kept on talking to him until he fell asleep again. "It's just a dream, baby. Just a dream."

*It had to be.*

Sunlight. And, with it, what passes for reason—a desperate groping for solace.

I'd only dreamed about the woman, imagined the rustling skirt; and Richard had only had a nightmare. The rest was fancy, a disorder of the nerves. That was my conclusion as I shaved. It is amazing how much one is willing to distort belief in the name of reason; how little one is willing to trust the intuitions of the flesh.

A combination of things served to bolster my conclusion. The aforementioned sunlight—always a strong factor in enabling one to deny the fears of the night. Add to that a tasty breakfast, a sunny-countenanced wife, a happy, laughing baby son, the first day of a week's work, and you have arrayed a potent force against belief in all things that have no form or logic.

By the time I left the house I was convinced. I walked across the street and up the alley beside Frank and Elizabeth's house; it was Frank's turn to drive. I knocked on the back door and went into their kitchen. Frank was still at the table, drinking coffee.

"Up, man," I said, "we'll be late."

"That's what you always say," he said. "Are we ever late?"

"Often," I answered, winking at Elizabeth who was standing at the stove.

"False," said Frank, "false as hell." He got up and stretched, groaning. "Oh, God," he said, "I wish it was Saturday." He walked out of the kitchen to get his suit coat. I asked Elizabeth how she was.

"Fine, thank you," she said. "Oh, we'd like you and Anne to come to dinner Wednesday night if you're free."

I nodded. "Fine. We'd love to." Elizabeth smiled and we stood there a moment in silence.

"That was certainly interesting the other night," she said then.

"Yes," I said. "Too bad I didn't get to see it."

She laughed faintly. "It was certainly interesting," she said.

Frank came back in.

"Well, off to goddamn Siberia," he said disgustedly.

"Darling, don't forget to bring home some coffee when you—" Elizabeth started to say.

"Hell, *you* get it," Frank interrupted angrily. "You've got all day to horse around. I'm not going shopping after working all day in that lousy, goddamn plant."

Elizabeth smiled feebly and turned back to the stove, a flush rising in her cheeks. I saw her throat move convulsively.

"Women," Frank said, jerking open the door. *"Jesus!"*

I didn't say anything. We left the house and drove to work. We were seven minutes late.

It happened that afternoon.

I'd just come out of the washroom. I stopped at the cooler and drew myself a cup of water. I drank it and, crumpling the cup, threw it into the disposal can. I turned and started back for my desk.

*And staggered violently as something heavy hit me on the head.*

At my cry, several of the men and women in the office turned suddenly from their work and gaped at me. My legs were rubbery under me and I was lurching sideways toward one of the desks; which I caught at desperately and clung to, a dazed expression on my face.

One of the men, Ken Lacey, ran over to me and caught me by the arm.

"What is it, fella?" I heard him ask.

"Anne," I said.

"What?"

*"Anne!"* I pulled away from him, then staggered again, my hands pressing at the top of my head. I could feel terrible shooting pains there; as if someone had hit me with a hammer.

Several other people came hurrying over.

"What is it?" I heard one of the secretaries say.

"I don't know," Lacey said. "Somebody get him a chair."

"Anne." I looked around with an expression of panic on my face. I wouldn't sit down.

"I'm all right, I'm all right," I kept insisting, managing to pull away from Lacey again. They watched me in surprise as I ran to my desk, threw myself down on the chair and grabbed the phone. They told me later I looked like a very frightened man. I was. The only trouble was I didn't know what I was frightened about. I only knew it had something to do with Anne.

The phone kept ringing at home with no one answering. I writhed in the chair and (they said later) the tense, stricken look on my face got worse. I punched down the button and dialed again with shaking fingers. I didn't look over to where they were standing, watching. I kept the receiver pressed to my ear.

"Come on," I remember muttering in an agony of inexplicable dread. "Come on. Answer!"

I heard the phone picked up.

"Hello?"

"Anne?"

"Is this you, Tom?" I recognized Elizabeth's thin voice and I felt as if someone had kicked me in the stomach.

*"Where's Anne?"* I said, barely able to breathe.

"She's on the bed," Elizabeth told me. "I just found her unconscious on the kitchen floor."

"Is she all right?"

"I don't know. I called the doctor."

"I'll be right there." I slammed down the receiver and jerked my coat off the hatrack. I must have looked like a maniac as I raced out of there.

The next half hour was sheer hell. I had to rush to Frank's department to get the car key—and that took a pass. Then I had to get another emergency pass to leave the plant. I raced across the parking lot until I got a stitch in my side—and, naturally, Frank had parked as far from the gate as it was possible to get. I gunned the car across the lot at sixty miles an hour, screeching to a halt at the gate, showed my pass, then jolted into the street.

It was pure luck I didn't get arrested at least a dozen times on that drive home. I passed red lights, stop signs, blinkers. I passed on the right, turned left from the right-hand lane and right from the left-hand lane; I broke every speed law there is. But I got home in twelve minutes.

I skidded to a halt and was out of the car before the motor sound had faded. I raced across the lawn, leaped onto the porch and slammed through the front doorway.

I found them in the bedroom, Anne on the bed, Elizabeth sitting beside her. Richard slipped off the bed as I entered and ran to me.

"Hi, daddy!" he said, cheerfully.

"Hello, baby." I stroked his head distractedly and moved quickly to the bed. Elizabeth got up and I sat where she'd been.

Anne smiled weakly at me. Her eyes didn't seem to focus very well. I saw that Elizabeth had put the ice-bag on her head.

"Are you all right, honey?" I asked.

Anne swallowed slowly and smiled again. "I'm all right." She more framed the words with her lips than spoke them aloud.

"Where's the doctor?" I asked Elizabeth.

"He hasn't come yet," she told me.

"Well . . . where in God's name is he?" I muttered. I looked back at Anne. "What happened?" I asked. "No, no, never mind. Don't talk. You're sure you're all right? You don't want me to take you to the hospital?"

"No." Her head stirred slightly on the pillow.

"Daddy, mama faw down." Richard was by my side now, looking at me very intently. For a second I seemed to see Anne standing in the kitchen, reaching upward—

"Yes, baby, I know," I said, putting my arm around him. I looked back at Anne. "You're sure you're all right?"

"It's all right." Her voice was a little clearer.

"How long ago did you call the doctor?" I asked Elizabeth.

"Just a few minutes before you called," she said.

"How did it happen?" I asked. "Did she faint?"

"I came over to say hello," Elizabeth said. "I found Anne on the kitchen floor. I think a large can of tomatoes fell off the top shelf and hit her."

I stared at her blankly. Then I turned to Anne.

"On . . . the top of your head?" I asked, slowly.

Her lips moved. "Yes."

The doctor came about three and said that the only complication was a big goose egg on Anne's skull. I phoned the plant and said I wouldn't be back. Elizabeth said she'd pick up Frank at four-fifteen.

A little before five o'clock Anne insisted she was all right and got up to make supper. While she was at the stove I sat at the table with Richard on my lap and told her what had happened.

She stopped stirring and looked over at me strangely.

"But that's fantastic," she said.

"I know it is. But it happened."

She stood there motionlessly, staring at me.

"No, why bother telling him?" I said.

Her face went blank. "What?" she asked.

"I said why bother telling him?"

"Telling who?"

"You just said we should—tell Phil," I said, "didn't you?"

"Tom, I didn't say anything."

There was a hanging pause. "You didn't?" I finally said.

"No."

I swallowed. I leaned back against the wall, hearing Richard tell me about a worm he and Candy had found in the back yard; not aware of the fact that I could see, in my mind, the actual scene of the two children kneeling on the soil, bent over, staring intently at the wriggling coils of the worm.

"What next?" I murmured. "Good God, what next?"

The dream again. Waking up with a gasp of terror, staring at the blackness, knowing she was in the living room waiting for me. Wanting to shout *Get out of here!* Burrowing under the covers instead, pressing close to Anne, shaking and terrified. Hearing the sound of a rustling skirt in the hallway, rushing to Richard once again as he woke up, crying. And, in the morning, another, dull, clinging headache, another stomach ache. A sense of depletion—of having been used. And the inevitable attempt to convince myself it was only a dream.

Futile now.

# SIX

WHEN I GOT HOME FROM WORK Tuesday afternoon I put the bag on the kitchen table.

"What's that?" Anne asked after we'd kissed.

"The sugar," I said.

She looked at me a moment.

"Do I dare ask," she said, "how you knew we needed sugar?"

"You didn't ask me to get it?" I asked, already knowing the answer.

Anne shook her head. "Well," she said, "maybe this thing will come in handy after all." It was a poor attempt at a joke.

I put the box of sugar in the cupboard and took off my suit coat.

"Hot," I said.

"Yes."

Anne started to set the table and I stood by the

kitchen window watching Richard and Candy run in erratic circles as they chased a butterfly.

"Tom?" I heard Anne say. I looked back. "What are you going to do?"

"You mean about—?" I couldn't find the word for it.

She nodded.

I sighed. "What is there to do?" I asked. "It's not something you can put your finger on. I dream about a strange woman." I hadn't told her yet that I didn't believe it was a dream. "I—think I can sense what's in Elsie's mind. I feel the same impact on my head that you do. I—pick up some of your thoughts about us needing sugar." I shrugged. "What do I have there to work with? How do I start?"

"You could go see Alan Porter," she said.

"There's nothing wrong with my mind," I said, turning away and looking out the window again.

"Well, what do you call it?" she asked. "It's happening in your mind, isn't it?"

"Yes, but it isn't a—a breakdown. If anything—" I paused a moment, realizing something. "If anything it's an increase, not a decrease."

"Does that make you feel better about it?" she asked. "You're frightened, Tom. Admit it. I can feel how you shiver at night when you have that dream. Call it anything you like. What matters is that all it's done is disturb you. And I think you should do something about it. Soon."

"All right," I said, uncertainly, "I'll . . . do something." I felt as if I were being forced into an undesirable corner, though. Certainly I was afraid of what was happening to me. Yet I was intrigued by it too.

All day at work I'd kept picking up fragments of thought and emotion from the people around me in the office. Scraps of feeling—irritation, boredom, weariness, daydreams, sexual and otherwise, wish fantasies. Vague disjointed visions and parts of phrases. I didn't know which person was thinking what, but that only enhanced the fascination.

One of them, for instance, was imagining himself—or herself on an ocean voyage that he—or she—had been on or wanted to be on. I swear I could almost smell the sea air and feel the roll of a ship under me. Another one was thinking of some woman and the vision was strained and ugly; tinged with the same overtones of what I'd sensed in Elsie's mind. It was a little sickening, yes, but still intriguing.

I turned from the window as an idea occurred to me.

"I wonder," I began.

"Now what?"

"I wonder if I've become—or if I'm becoming a medium."

"A *medium?*" Anne put down a bottle of milk hard.

"Yes," I said, "why not?" The expression on her face made me smile. "Honey, a medium doesn't have to be a lumpy, middle-aged woman in a button sweater, you know," I told her.

"I know but—"

"Well, think about it," I said. "The word itself—medium—is a perfect description. It means a—middle place. That's what mediums are. They stand between the—the source and the goal, letting thoughts and impressions flow through them. They—"

"If you're a medium," she broke in, "just tell me one thing."

"What?"

She looked at me intently, accusingly.

"Why haven't you got any control over what's flowing through *you?*"

\*       \*       \*

This continued to be the topic of our conversation at supper—interspaced with enjoining and commands to Richard to eat his food.

"No, I *don't* understand," Anne said. "You've been suffering with this thing. I can see a change in you already—yes, in just a few days," she insisted when I started to contest it. "You're pale. You're worn, tired."

"I know," I said. I couldn't argue. There were the headaches and the feeling of lead-boned weariness that followed every exposure to it.

"Well, I can't see it then," Anne said, irritated at my apparent reversal of attitude. "You agree it's hurting you and yet you tell me you don't want to do anything about it. Because you think you're a medium, or something."

"Honey, I'm not saying that," I said. "What I'm saying is that I want to see where it's going for a while. It is going somewhere; I feel it."

"Oh . . . feel, feel." She pressed her lips together angrily. "And what am I supposed to do at night when you jolt out of a sound sleep as if you'd been shot? I'm pregnant, Tom. I'm nervous too; *real* nervous. Do you think it's going to help me to be exposed to that every night?"

"Honey, I—"

The doorbell rang then and I got up and walked across the living room, wondering why I was feeling that tingling sensation. It was brief but most decided. While it lasted it was as if I were metallic and had passed into, then out of, a strong magnetic field.

I opened the door and saw Harry Sentas standing there.

"Oh." I was surprised. "Hello."

"Evening," he said. He was a tall, heavy-set man who, somehow, always looked unsuited to the clothes he wore. He would have looked more natural in overalls and a cap; maybe a grease stain across his florid cheek.

"I come to get the rent," he said. "Figured I'd save you a trip over."

"Oh." I nodded.

"Who there?" Richard came padding into the room and I heard Anne call him back.

"Well, isn't it two days yet?" I asked Sentas.

"Figured you'd wanna get it out of your hair before then," he said.

"I see." I cleared my throat. "Well, if you want to wait, I'll go make out a check."

"I'll wait," he said.

I went back into the kitchen and got the checkbook out of the cupboard drawer. Anne looked questioningly at me and I shrugged.

"Who that?" Richard asked.

"The man next door, baby," Anne said.

"Man ness door?"

I made out the check, tore it out of the book and brought it to Sentas.

"Obliged," he said, taking it.

"Oh, incidentally," I said, "I wonder if you'd get this door lock fixed."

"Door lock?"

"Yes. It can't be locked from the outside. When we leave the house we have to lock it from the inside and leave the patio door open."

"Oh?" he said. "I'll see about it."

"We'd appreciate it," I told him as he turned away and stepped over the plants onto the lawn. I watched him a moment walking toward his house. Then I shut the door and returned to my supper.

"Is this going to happen every month?" Anne said. "I thought it was an accident the first two times."

"I don't know." I shook my head. "I don't like it, though."

Anne shrugged. "He's just worried about his money, I suppose."

"His wife's money," I said. "According to Frank she's the one that's loaded."

She smiled, shaking her head. "Good old Frank," she said. "Always has a good word for everybody."

I exhaled. "Well, I don't like Sentas," I said.

Anne looked up from her plate. "Is this your— medium business?" she asked.

"Honey, you make me sound like some kind of freak."

"Well, I'd say it's a little freakish, wouldn't you?"

"Feakish," Richard said, "feakish, mama."

"Yes, baby," she said.

"Well, I don't regard myself as a freak," I said.

"Oh, come on," she said. "Let's not be so sensitive about it."

"You're the one that's sensitive."

"Don't you think I have some reason to be?" she asked, irritably.

"I know it's hard on you but—"

"But you're getting a bang out of it, so that's that."

"Honey, let's not argue," I said. "Look. I'll let it go on a little while longer. I promise you if it gets on your nerves, if it frightens you or anything, I'll—I'll go to Alan Porter. Is that fair enough?"

"Tom, it's *you* that's getting frightened and nervous."

"Well . . . I'm willing to stick it out a while longer," I told her. "I confess it makes me curious. Doesn't it you?"

She hesitated before answering. Finally she inclined her head in a grudging gesture.

"Oh, it's . . . unusual, all right," she said, "but . . .

well, if it throws our whole life out of balance, is it worth it?"

"I won't let it do that," I said. "You know that."

Before we went to sleep that night, we came across something that provided a definite clue.

I'd asked Anne to try and remember what had happened during the hypnosis and whether Phil had said anything that might have started me off.

She remembered two things. Neither was definite, of course; you never do find anything definite in something like this. But both were highly suggestive.

One remark was made when I was reliving segments of my twelfth year. Phil had said, in answer to somebody's question, "No, there's no limit to what his mind can do. It's capable of anything."

The second remark came when Phil was bringing me out of the hypnosis—and here, to me, was the key.

"Your mind is free now," he'd said to me. "There's nothing binding it. It's free, absolutely free."

It's something he'd said a hundred times before to hypnotized subjects. As I understand it, it's a command designed to prevent the subject's mind from retaining any suggestions inadvertently given which might later prove harmful. As I say, Phil had used it a hundred times; he verified that later.

Yet, for some reason, with me it had backfired.

I sat up with a gasp and felt the cold night air pressing at my sweat-streaked face; felt my heart pounding as I stared frozenly toward the living room.

She was in there again.

I sat there rigidly, my stomach muscles cramped and twitching, trying to make myself get up and go in there. But I couldn't. Will power was swept away. I saw her in my mind and it was more than I could do to get up, walk in there and find her, white and still, staring at me with her dark eyes.

*"Again?"*

I started with a frightened grunt and my heart leaped so hard it seemed to jolt against the wall of my chest. Then I swallowed with effort and drew in a long, shaking breath.

"Yes," I muttered.

"And . . . she's in there?"

"Yes. Yes."

I felt her shudder against me.

"Tom," she said and there was something different in her voice; something that didn't question. "Tom, what does she want?"

"I don't know," I answered as if, all along, we had both accepted the woman as objective reality.

"She's—still there?"

"Yes."

"Oh . . ." I thought I heard her sob and I reached out to touch her. I felt her hand against her mouth. She was biting the heel of it—hard.

"Anne, Anne," I whispered, "it's all right. She can't hurt us."

She pulled away her hand. Her voice broke over me in the darkness.

"What are you *doing* here?" she asked. "Are you just going to lie here and let this thing go on? If she's really in there, if she's what you say she is . . ."

I think we both stopped breathing at the same time. I stared at the dark outline of her, feeling my heart thud slowly, draggingly.

"Anne?" I heard myself murmur.

"What?"

"Don't . . . don't you believe what Phil said? That it's—"

"Do *you* believe it?"

I felt my hands shaking and I couldn't answer her.

Because suddenly I realized that I didn't believe what Phil had said. That I'd never believed him. It wasn't telepathy; it was something more.

But what?

# SEVEN

**A**RE YOU GOING TO TELL FRANK AND Elizabeth about it?" It was almost five on Wednesday; we were in the bedroom. Anne was sitting on the bed brushing Richard's hair, and I was putting on a fresh shirt. In a few minutes we'd be going across the street for dinner.

I slipped the sport shirt over my head, then stood looking at their reflection in the bureau mirror.

"Are you?" she asked.

I shook my head.

"No, why bother?" I said. "Frank would laugh at the whole thing."

It was quiet then. I knew what Anne was thinking. I'd been thinking the same thing. I also knew she didn't want to think it. I didn't want to either. It was too important. And, really, we had no right to dwell on it. What did we have for evidence? A shapeless feeling in the dead of night. The flash of an instinct, a brief second during which the yearning to believe in something beyond seemed to have become a realization, an acceptance. That wasn't enough; not enough at all.

I turned and leaned against the edge of the bureau. Anne avoided my eyes.

"Pitty shirt, daddy," Richard said.

"Thank you, baby," I said.

"Weckome," Richard said; and, for a moment, something seemed to pass between us; a sort of understanding. Then he had turned away.

I looked at him and thought how much easier it would be to raise him if I could only believe. All those ever-present dreads would be ameliorated—fatal illness, being run down by a car, being killed by any one of the myriad accidents to which a child is so horribly vulnerable. I thought how wonderful it would be if I could believe that he was safe.

For a moment Anne's eyes met mine.

"I do know one thing," I said impulsively. "There's something around us. I don't know what it is but it's something. And it's there, Anne. It's *there*."

I remember the look she gave me. How, for a moment, she pressed her lips to Richard's white-blond hair.

"It would be so nice," she said, almost to herself, "so nice."

Frank let us in.

"Greetings, fellow sufferers," he slurred. His beer-sweet breath fogged over us. "Hobble the hell on in."

As we entered the living room, Elizabeth came out of the kitchen. It wasn't hard to tell they'd been fighting. Even if I hadn't sensed the swelling of tension in the air, I could see that Elizabeth had been crying.

"Hello." She came toward us, forcing a smile, not looking at Frank. "Hello, dear," she said to Richard.

Frank caught her around the waist as she came up to us and I saw his white fingers dig into the soft flesh of her stomach.

"This is my wife, Lizzie," he said. "Lizzie, mother of my unborn brat."

Elizabeth pulled away with a pained grimace and stooped down before Richard. . . . *hate!* . . . The word seemed to flare in my mind the way a bulb does just before it has burned out and gone black.

"You look so handsome, Richard," she said. There was a break in her voice. "That's a pretty suit."

"Never tells me *I'm* handsome," Frank said.

"Pitty?" Richard plucked at the shirt and held the bright material out toward Elizabeth.

"Oh, yes. So pretty."

"Well, sittenzie down, guests," said Frank, "and name your poison—to quote the immortal lines of that world-famous bitch, Elsie Leigh."

"You are in a good mood," I told him.

"What, goddammit, is your pleasure, goddammit?" Frank said.

"Nothing for me," Anne said stiffly. I said a glass of wine if he had some. He named off three. I said sauterne.

"*Saw*-terne—coming goddamn up." Frank lurched away toward the kitchen with a belch.

Elizabeth straightened up, a strained smile on her face.

"He's had a bad day," she said, trying in vain to make it sound amusing. "Don't pay any attention to him."

"Are you sure you want to bother with us, Liz?" Anne asked softly. "We wouldn't mind if—"

"Oh, don't be silly, dear," Elizabeth said and I sensed a wave of taut unhappiness rushing through her. In the kitchen Frank belched again ringingly. "Key of C," he said.

"Oh . . . before I forget," Elizabeth said, "did I leave a comb at your house the other day?"

Anne clucked. "For heaven's sake," she said. "Yes. You did. I've been meaning to bring it back at least a dozen times and I keep forgetting. I'm sorry."

"Oh, that's all right, dear," Elizabeth said. "I just want to know where it is. I'll pick it up sometime."

"*Saw*-terne." Frank came back in the room with a filled glass in his hand.

"I'll get dinner ready," Elizabeth said, starting for the kitchen.

"Let me help you," Anne offered.

"There's nothing to do," Elizabeth said, smiling. The smile faded. Frank was blocking her way. "Frank," she said, pleadingly.

"Lizzie doesn't talk here any more," he said. "Do you, Lizzie?"

"Frank, let me by." Her voice was strained.

"Oh, she's so mad, so mad." He pawed at her shoulder. "You mad there, Lizzie?"

"I'll help you, Liz," Anne said, getting up and taking Richard's hand. Elizabeth opened her mouth as if to speak, then didn't. I could sense the gratitude and anger mixed in her. Frank stepped aside as Anne came over and the two women and Richard started into the kitchen.

"One pregnant woman," itemized Frank, "one little boy. *Two* pregnant women." He blew out a whistling breath." 'Tis the season to be jolly." He snickered, "Pretty good, eh?" he asked me.

"Just as funny as it can be," I said.

"You don't think that, you sober bastard" he said. He handed me the glass roughly and some of the wine spilled up over the edge and across my hand. "Ooops," said Frank, "oops, oops."

He just about fell down on the arm chair.

"She's mad," he said, "just 'cause I told her to try and lift the refrigerator so we wouldn't have to bother having a kid." Chuckling, he reached for his can of beer. He held it out.

"Here's to un-knocked-up femininity," he toasted. "Long may the hell they wave." He hiccupped and drained the can. Abruptly his face grew flatly sullen. He dropped the empty can on the rug.

"Babies," he said, bitterly, loud enough to be heard in the kitchen. "Who the hell invented them?"

If I'd had any intention of telling them about the woman, Frank dispelled it quickly. He kept drinking until dinner was on the table and then kept on all through it, barely touching his food. It got to the point where, when Elizabeth—in a desperate search for diverting conversation—mentioned my strange phone call when Anne had been knocked unconscious, I shrugged and said it had only been a coincidence. I just didn't want to talk about it there.

I thought of the way mediums often describe their entrances into haunted houses—how they sense alien presences in the air. Well, that house was haunted too. I felt it strongly. Haunted by despairs, by the ghosts of a thousand cruel words and acts, by the phantom residue of unresolved angers.

"Babies," Frank kept saying as he stabbed vengefully at his food, "babies. Are they valid? Are they integral? Do they add up? Are they the goddamn sum of their parts? I ask you."

"Frank, you're making it—" Elizabeth started.

"Not you," he interrupted, "I'm not asking you. You're sick in the head about babies. Babies are your mania. You live babies, you breathe babies." He looked at Anne and me. "Lizzie," he said, "is baby happy. Alla time, alla time—'when we gonna make a baby?' 'When we gonna put sperm to egg?' and—"

*"Frank . . ."* Elizabeth's fork clinked onto her plate; she covered her eyes with a trembling hand. Richard stared at her, wide-eyed. Anne reached across the table and put her hand on Elizabeth's.

"Take it easy, man," I said. "You trying to give us indigestion or something?"

"Sure," Frank said. "Easy he says. Easy. You try to take it easy when something that isn't even alive yet eats up all your money."

He shook his head dizzily.

"Babies, babies, babies," he chanted. He glanced at me suddenly. "What are you looking at me for?" Superficials were gone. He looked at me as if he hated my guts.

I blinked and lowered my eyes. I hadn't been conscious of staring at him. I'd only been conscious of the twisted, angry wellings in his mind.

"Just looking at an idiot I know," I said.

He hissed in disgust.

"I'm an idiot, all right," he said. "Any guy's an idiot who makes babies."

"Frank, for God's *sake!*" Elizabeth pushed up from the table shakily and put her plate in the sink.

"Richard," said Frank, "don't make babies. Make girls. Make whoopee. Make trouble. But don't make babies."

The remainder of the meal, dessert and all, was eaten in a tense silence broken only by vain attempts at dinner conversation.

Later, Frank and I went out for a drive. He'd kept on drinking and was getting more and more abusive to Elizabeth so I suggested we go for a ride. I took our car so I could do the driving. I told him I had to get gas for the next day anyway.

"Don't matter," he said, "I'm not going to work anyhow. Why should I?"

As we pulled away from the curb Elsie came out of

the house in a sunsuit and waved to us, then bent over to pick up the hose.

"Fat bitch," Frank snapped. The impression I got from him was not one of anger, though—unless it was angry lust.

We drove in silence a while. Frank had rolled down the window on his side all the way and his head lolled out of it, the cold night wind whipping his dark hair. I kept my eyes straight ahead, heading toward the ocean. Once in a while Frank muttered something but I paid no attention. I kept thinking about life going on, every little realism driving one farther from any thinking about the other things.

Once we'd seen a hypnotist on television. He had a young woman in a trance and she was very calmly giving him facts and figures about her former life in Nuremburg in the 1830s.

At first I'd been glued to the chair, absolutely spell-bound. The woman talked fluent German even though she was American for four generations back; she described buildings and people; she gave dates, addresses, names.

Then, as I watched, the little realities began to impinge. I felt the bump in the chair cushion I was sitting on. My head itched. I was thirsty and I took a sip of Coca-Cola from the glass on the magazine-strewn coffee table in front of me. I heard the rustle of Anne's clothes as she shifted her weight beside me on the sofa. I became aware of the smallness of the television tube in relation to the room. I heard an airplane pass overhead and noted the books in the bookcase. And this woman went on talking and talking and gradually this incredible thing became ordinary and dull. I sank back against the sofa back and watched without too much interest. I even changed to another channel before it was over.

It was the same way now. Feeling the hard seat

under me, the steering wheel in my hands, the sound of the Ford's engine in my ears, seeing, from the corner of my eye, Frank sitting there glumly, seeing the lights flashing by—it was all too real; too matter-of-fact. Everything else seemed unacceptable. The woman was, once again, a dream. And all the rest— even to the sensing of Frank's and Elizabeth's thoughts—seemed imaginative fancy. Something to be explained away.

After driving about twenty minutes we stopped at a bar in Redondo Beach and sat in a back booth, drinking beer. Frank drained three glasses quickly before dawdling over the fourth. He rubbed the ice-sweated bottom of the glass over the smooth table top and stared at it.

"What's the use?" he said, without looking at me.

"Use of what?" I asked.

"Use of everything," he said. "Marriage and kids and all the rest of it." His cheeks puffed out with held breath, then he expelled it noisily. "I suppose you want a baby," he said.

"Sure."

"You would." He drank a little beer.

"I take it you don't," I said.

"You take it right, buddy boy," he said bitterly. "Sometimes I'd like to kick her right in the goddamn belly just so she'd . . . *uh*—" He squeezed the glass in his hand as if he wanted to splinter it. "What good is a baby to me?" he asked. "What the hell do I want with one?"

"They're pretty nice," I said.

He fell back against the booth wall. "Sure," he said, "sure. So's a little money in the bank. So's a little security."

"They don't eat money, Frank," I said, "just a little mush and milk."

"They eat money," he said, "just like wives eat

money. Just like houses and furniture and goddamn curtains."

"Man, you sound like a frustrated bachelor," I told him.

"A frustrated husband," he said. "I wish to hell I *was* a bachelor. Them, buddy, was the goddamn days."

"They were all right," I said, "but I'll take these."

"You can have 'em," he growled. He blew out disgusted breath again and played with his glass. "Isn't bad enough," he muttered, "I have to practically beg her for some when she's normal. Now she's got a whole goddamn bag full of tricks she uses to kick me out of bed."

I guess I laughed. "Is that what's bothering you?" I asked. I didn't feel very telepathic at that moment. It caught me by surprise.

"You bet your goddamn life it bothers me," Frank said. "She has the sex drive of a goddamn butterfly. Even when she's normal. Now . . ."

"Frank," I said, "believe me, pregnancy is not abnormal."

"The hell it isn't," he said. "It's a waste of flesh." He leaned forward and his face was hard and intent. "Well, buddy boy," he said, "I'm not taking it lying down." He snickered. "To use the vernacular." He looked around in the way men do to indicate that their next remarks are going to be shattering revelations.

"There's a little redheaded job at the plant," he said.

I was surprised again.

"Oh, she knows about it," he said. "Old Lizzie knows all about it. What the hell else can she expect, though? A man needs it. That's all. And I need a lot of it. It's a matter of simple arithmetic."

He went on telling me about the little "job"—

redheaded, petite, tight-sweatered and sheathed with hugging slacks. She brought papers to the accounting department and dropped them off there.

"I don't get much eating done at lunchtime," Frank said, winking.

# EIGHT

**I** CAN'T STAND HIM," ANNE TOLD ME AS we were getting ready for bed that night. "He's loathsome. He's got that poor woman on the verge of a nervous breakdown."

I pulled off my second sock and dropped it into my shoe.

"I know," I said.

"All she wants is a baby," Anne said. "God! You'd think she was asking for the moon! She doesn't ask a thing of him; not a *thing*! He doesn't help her with anything! He goes out by himself whenever he damn well pleases. He begrudges her every cent she spends no matter how carefully she budgets. He yells at her and abuses her. I've seen black and blue marks on that girl—*bad* ones."

She slung the hanger over the closet bar. "And she doesn't say a thing," she said. "All she wants is a baby.

Seven years of marriage and that's all she asks. And *him* . . ."

"Maybe that's her trouble," I said. "She lets him get away with too much."

"What can she do?" Anne asked, sitting down at her dressing table and picking up her brush.

"Leave him?" I suggested.

"Where would she go?" she asked, brushing with short, angry strokes. "She hasn't a friend in the world. Both her parents have been dead for nine years. If you and I ever broke up, I, at least, could go home to my mother and father for a while to get over it. Elizabeth hasn't a place in the world to go. That's her home over there. And that—pig is making it a hell."

I sighed. "I know," I said. I lay back on the bed. "I wonder, does she really know he's having an affair with—?"

I stopped. I could tell from the way her head had snapped around what the answer was.

"He's *what?*" she asked, slowly.

We looked at each other a moment. She turned away.

"That's fine," she said in that falsely calm voice a woman manages to achieve when she is at the height of her fury. "That's just fine. That really ices the cake. That really does."

I smiled without amusement.

"So she doesn't know," I said. "He said she did."

"Oh, he's—he's a . . . there isn't any word bad enough." I shook my head slowly.

"That's a real nice situation there," I said. "I feel like a soap-opera character living in this house. On one side we have a wife who kicks the guts out of her husband. On the other side we have an adulterer and a drudge." I got under the covers. "I wouldn't tell her if I were you."

"Tell her?" Anne said. "Good God, I wouldn't dare. If anything could snap her right down the middle, that'd be it."

She shivered.

"Tell her. Oh . . . God, not me. I shudder to think what'll happen if she finds out."

"She won't," I said.

We were quiet a while. I lay there looking at the ceiling, wondering if I was going to have that dream again—mentally feeling around the house; as if my thoughts were insect antennae quivering, searching timidly, ready to recoil in an instant at the slightest touch of anything.

But there was nothing. I began to think that maybe the keyed-up state Phil had left me in really was fading; that I was, already, below the level of awareness, and now it would keep sinking until I was as I had been before. Frankly, it made me feel a little disappointed. It *was* an intriguing capacity. I found myself almost straining to revitalize it in myself. Of course it didn't work. It wasn't voluntary.

A few minutes later, Anne got in bed beside me and we turned out the lights.

"You—think you're going to dream tonight?" she asked.

"I don't know," I said. "I don't think so, though."

"Maybe it's gone."

"Could be."

Silence a while.

"Honey?" she said then.

"Yes?"

I heard her swallowing.

"About . . ."

"About last night?" I asked.

"Yes. I—I'm sorry I let myself get out of hand."

"It's nothing to be sorry about, honey."

"Yes, it is," she said. "It's pointless to think about

such things just because of—what's happened."

"I guess," I said. I rolled onto my side and put my arm over her.

"You—promise we—"

"All right," I said, "we won't talk about it."

"I—just don't think it's—sensible," she said.

"I suppose not," I said.

She kissed my cheek. "Good night, honey," she said.

"Good night," I said. On the bedside table, the radium-faced clock read eleven-thirty.


"No!"

I wrenched up from the mattress, awareness razoring in my mind. My eyes were wide open, stiffly set. I stared toward the living room.

Anne had jolted awake with me. I heard her now, her voice shaking.

*"Again?"* she asked.

"Yes. Y-es."

"Oh . . . no. *No.*" She sounded almost angry.

We sat there a few moments. I could feel my chest rising and falling with fitful motion, the breath gushing out through my nostrils. My lips were sealed together, my heart thudded harshly, off-time.

"What are you going to do?" she asked. There was a scared, embittered challenge in her voice.

"What—can I do?"

She drew in a rasping breath.

*"Get up and see."*

I twisted around. "Honey, what is it?"

"What is it? What kind of question is that? You know what it is. Now get up—" A sobbing broke her voice. *"Get up and go in there."*

Breath shuddered in me. I felt myself shaking helplessly. Every time I thought about the woman she seemed to flare into strengthened clarity in my mind—

white-faced and staring, her dark eyes asking for something.

I caught my breath.

"All right," I said. I don't know if I was talking to Anne or to the woman. "All right." I snapped aside the covers and dropped my legs over the side of the bed.

"Honey." The anger was suddenly gone from her voice. Only concerned fear remained.

"What?" I asked.

"I . . . I'll go with you."

I swallowed dryly. "You stay," I said.

"No, I—I want to. I want to."

I rubbed a shaking hand over my face and drew away cold sweat. I knew I should make her stay.

"All right," I heard myself saying. "Come on then."

I heard the liquid rustle of her nightgown as she got up. I saw the dark outline of her figure against the window. I stood and we came together at the foot of the bed. I felt her hand clutch at mine and I grabbed it tightly. It was cold and dry; it trembled in my grip.

I took a deep breath and tried to stop the shaking of my stomach muscles. They were tight and cramped again. I felt that hot, needling pulse at my temples.

"All right," I said. "Come on."

Did ever two people stalk the darkness more slowly? We moved as if our legs were lead, as if we were statues come only half alive. We edged to the door in whispers of movement; and all the time my heart kept beating faster and faster and I thought I could almost hear the beat of it. My hand shook now too. It was no comforting strength to her. How can there be comfort from a frightened man?

We reached the hall and stopped as if by mutual consent. Between us and the living room was a door. We stood there shivering in the darkness; then jolted with shock as, in the other bedroom, Richard stirred a little. Then I heard Anne's voice, barely audible.

*"Open it,"* she said.

I set myself. I gripped her hand until I'm sure it must have hurt her.

Abruptly, I kicked open the door.

We both recoiled automatically, braced for the worst.

Then it all seemed to drain away with a sudden recession. Our hands fell apart.

We walked into the empty living room. The tingling in my head was fading, the knots untying in my stomach.

I saw Anne lean against the wall.

"You bastard," she said clearly and there was only amused relief in her shaky voice. "Oh, you double-dyed bastard."

I swallowed.

*"Honey,* I . . . thought she was in here."

"Sure you did, ducky," she said. "Sure you did." Her hand patted me and I felt how it shook.

She took a deep breath.

"Well," she said, "shall we retire?" I knew from the sound of her voice that she would have screamed her lungs out if we'd seen anything.

"In a moment," I said.

She went back to bed. I heard her climb under the covers and heard her say, "Come on, Madame Wallace."

"Right away."

I went to bed and lay quietly beside her. I didn't tell her about the cold, damp breeze that had passed over me as I'd turned from the living room.

# NINE

"WELL, I GOT US A BABY-SITTER FOR tonight," Anne told me cheerfully when I got home Thursday afternoon. I lowered my gurgling son from my shoulder and put him on the floor. I kissed my wife.

"Good," I said. "Fine. We can use a night out after what we've been through."

*"Amen,"* she said. "I feel as if I've done ten years' field work for the Psychical Research Society."

I laughed and patted her. "And how's the little mother?" I asked.

"A lot better now, thank you, Mr. Medium."

"Call me that again and I'll punch you right in the belly," I said.

It was a forced joke. I couldn't tell her about the dull headache I'd had all day, the small stomach ache, the continuing of awareness. She was too happy for me to start it again. And, for that matter, I wasn't certain. As always, it was vague and undefined. And I was damned if I was going to bring up *feelings* again.

"Who's the sitter?" I asked while I was washing up for supper.

"The girl Elsie told us about," Anne said. "She's really a deal too. Only charges fifty cents an hour."

"How about that?" I said. I thought about it a moment. "You sure she's reliable?"

"You remember what Elsie said about her," Anne said. " 'Real reliable.' "

I remembered.

I drove over to get the girl a little before eight. She lived about four miles from our house which wasn't too satisfactory but we'd been looking for a baby-sitter a long time and I wasn't going to quibble. We needed a night out badly.

I braked in front of the girl's house and started to get out when the front door opened and she came out. She was heavy and the tight blue jeans she wore did nothing to conceal it. She was wearing a brown leather jacket and there was a faded yellow ribbon like a streak of butter through the drabness of her brunette hair. She wore shell-rim glasses.

I pushed open the door and she slid in beside me and pulled the door shut.

"Hello," I said.

"Hello." Her voice was faint. She didn't look at me. I released the hand brake, checked the rear-view mirror, then made a fast U-turn and started back.

"My name's Tom Wallace," I said.

She didn't reply.

"Your name's Dorothy?"

"Yes." I could hardly hear her.

I drove a few blocks before I glanced over at her. She was staring straight ahead at the road, looking very somber. I'm not sure but I think it was at that moment I began to feel uncomfortable.

"What's your last name?" I asked. I didn't hear what she mumbled. "What was that?" I asked.

"Muller," she said.

"Oh. Uh-huh." I signaled, turned right onto Hawthorne Avenue and picked up speed again.

"Have you sat for Elsie long?" I asked.

"Elsie Long?"

"No. I mean Elsie Leigh. Have you been baby-sitting for her very long?"

"No."

"I see." What was there about her that disturbed me? "I—uh—we were wondering if you had a time limit," I said. "We assumed that—"

"No," she interrupted.

"Oh. I thought maybe—with school and everything."

"No."

"I see. Your mother doesn't mind, then."

She didn't answer. Suddenly I seemed to get an impression in my mind—that she had no mother.

"Is your mother dead?" I asked, without thinking; or, rather, thinking aloud.

Her head turned quickly. In the darkness I could feel her eyes on me. I knew I was right even though she didn't speak.

I cleared my throat.

"Elsie mentioned it," I said, taking the risk that I was right as well as the risk that Elsie didn't even know about it.

"Oh." From the way she said it I couldn't tell if she'd spotted my lie or not. She looked at the road again. So did I. I drove the rest of the way without a word, wondering what it was I felt so uneasy about.

When we got to the house Dorothy got out of the car and walked to the front door. There she waited until I came up on the porch and opened it for her. I noticed how short she was.

"Go on in," I said, feeling a crawling sensation on my back as she walked past me into the living room. Somehow it made me angry. I'd hoped for a pleasant evening of forgetfulness with Anne. Now all the disturbances were beginning again—inexplicable and enraging.

Anne came out of Richard's room into the living room.

"Hi," she said.

Dorothy's lips twitched into a mechanical smile. I saw that her white, thick-featured face was dotted with tiny pimples.

"The baby's asleep," Anne told her. "You shouldn't have any trouble with him at all."

Dorothy nodded. And—suddenly—I felt a shocking burst of dismay in myself. It made me catch my breath. When it left—almost immediately—it left me limp.

"I'll be ready in a second," Anne said to me.

I forget what I answered except that it was said distractedly. Anne went back into the bathroom to brush her hair and Dorothy stood by the back window, near where I'd seen the woman. Momentarily, I felt that cold, knotting sensation in my stomach. I smiled nervously at the girl as she glanced at me. I gestured toward the bookcase.

"If you—uh—care to read anything," I said, "feel free to—"

Her eyes fell from mine. She still had her jacket zipped to the neck, her hands deep in the slash pockets.

"Take off your jacket, why don't you?" I said. She nodded without looking at me.

I gazed at her a moment. What I felt was—as it had always been—without definition; more a sense of vague, remote discomfort than anything else.

"Well, there's the television set," I said.

She nodded once more.

I went into the kitchen and got myself a drink of water. It tasted brackish to me. I remember pressing my lips together furiously, telling myself—Enough! You're going to enjoy yourself tonight if it kills you!

"If you get hungry," I called to Dorothy, "feel free to take whatever you want in the icebox."

No sound.

As I went back in she was just starting to take off her jacket. I caught a momentary glimpse of breast outline much too heavy for a girl her age. Then the jacket was off, her shoulders had moved back into normal position and the large blouse she wore had fallen into veiling looseness around her. A flush darkened her cheeks. I walked past her as if I hadn't noticed. I went into the bathroom and looked over Anne's shoulder into the mirror.

I smiled back at her reflection.

"You all right?" she asked.

"Sure. Why do you ask?"

"You looked a little peaked."

"I'm fine," I said. I drew a comb from my inside coat pocket and ran it through my hair. I wondered if she noticed the slight shaking of my hand. I wondered if she had any idea that I was considering the possibility I was losing my mind.

"Oh, Dorothy," Anne said as we were leaving.

"Yes." Dorothy got up from the sofa.

"You'll have to lock the door from the inside. We can't do it with a key."

"Oh." Dorothy nodded once.

"Well, good night," said Anne. "We'll see you later."

Dorothy grunted.

I cannot describe the crushing sensation I felt when

I heard the sound of the door being locked by Dorothy. For a moment I stood there rigidly, feeling my stomach muscles tighten. Then Anne took my arm and, forcing a smile for her sake, I escorted her to the car.

"Did I tell you you look gorgeous tonight?" I asked as I slid onto the front seat beside her.

She leaned over and kissed me lightly. "Kind sir," she said.

I held her a moment, breathing in the delicate fragrance of her perfume. By God, I vowed, I am going to stop this damned nonsense. Enough was enough.

"You smell good," I said.

"Thank you, darling."

Then I looked up toward the house and thought I saw Dorothy watching us through the parted blinds.

"Honey, what is it?" Anne asked.

I drew back, smiling; rather unconvincingly, I'm afraid. "What do you mean?" I asked.

"You positively twitched."

"Did I positively twitch, love?" I tried to cover up. "It is passion, it is desire."

She cocked her head a little.

"Oh so?" she said.

"Oh so, indeed," I said. "Don't think you can hide behind your condition."

"Well, you're the freshest damn chauffeur *I* ever hired," she said.

I grinned and started the engine. As we pulled away from the curb I glanced at the house again and this time there was no doubt; I definitely saw the blinds slip back into place. Something jerked in my stomach and I had the sudden impulse to jam on the brakes and go running back to the house. I actually had to fight the inclination. My foot jerked on the gas pedal and the car jolted a little.

"Easy does it, Barney Oldfield," Anne said.

"It is your presence, madame, that undoes my foot," I said and managed to keep from my voice the turmoil I felt. My hands would have shaken if they hadn't been clamped so tight over the steering wheel. Self-anger only made it worse.

"Oh, did you ask her if she has a time limit?" Anne asked.

"There isn't any," I answered, wishing immediately that I'd lied and said we had to be back at eleven—at ten.

"Wonderful," Anne said, as I'd feared, "we can enjoy ourselves without keeping one eye on the clock."

"Yeah." The charm failed this time. I couldn't keep what I felt out of my voice. Out of the corner of my eye I saw Anne look over at me as I turned onto the boulevard.

"That was a very inconclusive yeah," she said.

"Not at all, my—" I started, then stopped. I realized that it was Richard I was concerned about and Anne certainly couldn't object to that. If only I could put it in such a way that she wouldn't think it was the "telepathy business" again. I was actually beginning to get a guilt complex about it.

"Well," I said, hesitantly, "I . . . just feel a little dubious about staying out too late the first time. After all, Elsie's recommendation is hardly a national seal of approval."

"No," she said. "Well . . . we won't stay out past midnight. We can do a lot by then anyway."

*Midnight.* I clenched my teeth and sat there stiffly. That was no triumph at all. I still felt like going back and taking the girl home. But that was ridiculous.

I told myself.

We talked a while about where we were going, finally settling on The Lighthouse in Hermosa Beach because it was relatively close to home and also a nice place to have a few drinks and listen to some good modern jazz. That decided, conversation was taken up mainly by Anne while I drove and fretted.

"Honey, there *is* something wrong," Anne finally said in the middle of a sentence. "Don't you feel well?"

I realized that, as a matter of fact, the headache *was* getting worse. I could ignore that, however. That wasn't my concern at the moment.

"No, there's nothing wrong," I said, irritated at myself for feeling the need to lie. "I'm just—oh, a little worried about leaving Richard with that girl."

"Honey, Elsie said she was fine."

"I know. I—" I shrugged and smiled awkwardly. "I guess I sound like an old lady. I just want to feel sure about Richard, though."

"Honey, don't you think I do? I asked Elsie all sorts of questions about the girl. And I spoke to her father this afternoon before setting it up."

"Her mother's dead, isn't she?" I said.

"Yes. How did you know?"

I cleared my throat. "Dorothy told me," I said. I wished more and more that I could let out the whole damned business; tell Anne it hadn't gone away, that I was still picking up thoughts and feelings and I simply didn't trust the girl. I felt childishly secretive for not saying it. And yet, when I looked on the other side of the inconclusive coin, I knew I had just as much reason *not* to say it. If I did, I'd start another rise of panic in Anne and, very possibly, malign a girl whose only fault was being overweight. After all, hadn't I been wrong about the woman the night before?

Which helped not at all. That was the worst part of all this. Logic I could doubt. What I *felt*, I never really questioned. Beside which, I wasn't sure I had been wrong about the woman.

All this I kept mulling over while Anne told me

about Dorothy, my mind constantly oscillating between the foundation of reason and the fluidity of emotion. I'm afraid I didn't hear much.

She was fifteen; I heard that. She lived with her father and eight-year-old brother. She attended junior high and sat for several people. Her father also worked at North American; he was a welder on the night shift.

Nothing there to disturb me; but, of course, that didn't help. What disturbed me, now as always, was what was behind the fact—the emotion behind the word, the thought that lurked behind the barricades of silence. That was what had bothered me with Elsie and—

*Elsie!*

It suddenly occurred to me. The sick, revulsed feeling I'd gotten with Elsie—*it had been very similar to the sensation I'd gotten with Dorothy.*

For a few moments that made me feel better—*logically.* The cruel, enervating demands of puberty were not such a mystery—and not such a menace.

"So are you convinced, daddy?" Anne asked at the conclusion of her report on Dorothy.

I nodded. "I stand bowed," I said, "chastened. Heat up the humble pie. Onward to jazzland."

Anne laughed softly and shifted closer to me. She closed her hand over my leg.

"In-deed," she said.

I managed to convince myself that I wasn't concerned any more.

At least until we'd parked, gotten out of the car, walked to The Lighthouse, entered its quaint din, gotten a table near the piano side of the bandstand, ordered drinks and started listening to the delicate, atonal fancies of a piece called "Aquarium."

Then it started again.

Sitting there, my hand wrapped around the icy height of my vodka collins glass, staring at the ecstatic facial expressions of the writhing bass player, I started thinking about Dorothy.

Every thought was a cold dripping of premonition inside of me. What was it about her that was wrong? Why did I fear her? What could she do to hurt Richard? That was the crux of it, of course. What could she—?

Anne said something, breaking the chain of thought. The music was too loud, though, and I couldn't hear. I could tell from the expression on her face, however, approximately what it was. I leaned forward.

"Tom, what *is* it?" she asked, tensely.

I shook my head, smiling vaguely and she turned away. I looked at her. Dread kept piling up in me. Tell her, I thought. Tell her, for God's sake! Make a mistake if you have to—but don't just sit here like this—sick with fear.

I touched her arm and she turned.

I didn't say anything. For a long moment our eyes held and I knew she felt what flickered between us as surely as I did. Then, with a tightening of her lips, she drew on her topcoat and picked up her handbag.

When the door had swung shut behind us, cutting off the wild sound of music, she started for the car.

"Honey," I started to say.

"Never mind, Tom."

"Listen," I said irritably, "do you think this is for me?"

She made a little hopeless gesture with her right hand and didn't answer. When we reached the car she stood there waiting for me to unlock it. For a moment I was about to say something about being sorry, and going back to The Lighthouse. But I knew I couldn't. I unlocked the door quickly and she got in. I slammed the door and found myself running around the front of the car.

I started the motor and pulled away from the curb, gunning it. At the corner I had to stop sharply for a red light and it made me hiss impatiently. I knew Anne was looking at me but I couldn't look back. I began to sense that she knew what it was. Knowing that only increased the dismaying fear that was eating at me.

When the light changed I jammed my foot down on the accelerator and the Ford leaped forward and roared up the winding grade that led toward the coast highway.

Now that I'd given up trying to fight it, the dread mounted quickly. My mind seemed to flee ahead to the house. Abruptly, I was on the porch. I was in the living room and the lights were out. I was in the hall and there were no lights in the entire house. I made a frightened sound and Anne looked over at me quickly. I heard her start to say something, then stop. The Ford raked around the corner and headed north on the highway. I don't know what part of me paid attention to the driving. Most of me was in that house, searching, panic-stricken. Richard! I heard myself call out.

*Richard!*

The car never seemed so slow before. Sixty was a creep, fifty a drag, forty was standing still. Waiting for a light was an agony of prescience. I knew that Anne wanted to speak but didn't dare. I didn't want to speak; I only wanted to get home in a second.

By the time I pulled up in front of the house I was shaking. Switching off the engine, I shoved out the door and raced across the dark lawn, leaping onto the porch with one panicked bound. Behind me I heard the other door slam shut and the fast click of Anne's +following heels. I didn't even bother knocking. A single twist of the knob told me the door was still locked. Turning quickly, I ran past Anne as she started up the porch steps.

"Where are you going?" she asked.

"Back door," I gasped.

"There are no lights," she said in a falsely normal voice.

I didn't answer. I darted around the corner of the garage and sprinted up the alley.

The back door was wide open. I started in, then, abruptly, whirled and lunged out again, driven. Instinctively, I turned to the left and ran into the back yard.

She was cringing in a dark corner when I found her. In her arms, a blanket wrapped around him, was Richard.

Without a word I took him from her and turned away. A terrible, half-mad sound broke in Dorothy's throat. I didn't stop. I carried Richard toward Anne who was standing at the end of the alley.

"What is it?" she asked in a thin, frightened voice.

"Turn on the kitchen light," I told her.

Backing off, she turned and hurried into the house. The kitchen light flared on.

Anne gasped as I carried Richard in. "*No,*" she whimpered.

"He's all right," I said, quickly. "He didn't even wake up."

She followed me across the living room into the hall, turning on the lights. In his room, I set Richard down into the crib and unwound the blanket. Anne came in, a look of sick dread on her face.

"Is he—hurt?" she asked.

"I don't think so." I turned on the overhead light and Richard stirred fitfully. I seemed to feel a dread that was his. It was sinking away; gone in an instant. He began to snore peacefully.

"Oh, my God." She would have fallen if I hadn't caught her. I led her into the hall, bracing her with my arm, turning out the light in Richard's room as we left.

"It's all right," I said, "it's all right, Anne."

Her face was like wax. *"What if we hadn't come back?"* she whispered.

"We did come back," I said. "That's all that matters."

"Oh, Tom, Tom." She began shaking in my arms.

"It's all right," I told her.

I held her for several minutes. Then I said, "I better take her home."

"What?" She raised her head.

"The girl. She lives too far away to walk."

Anne swallowed, her lips trembling. "I'm calling the police," she said.

"No, no, no," I said, "it wouldn't do any good."

"Tom, this could happen again!" Anne said, looking terrified. "She'll try to kidnap someone else's child!"

"No, she won't," I said. "She's been sitting for Elsie all this time and never tried it. I don't know why she tried it tonight but I'm sure it won't happen again."

Anne shook her head. "I don't know," she said. "I don't know."

I tried to get her into bed but she wouldn't go. As I left the house she was standing in Richard's room, looking down at him.

Dorothy wasn't in the back yard. I went out to the street and looked toward the boulevard. Up on the next block I saw her walking erratically. I got into the car and followed her.

She kept stumbling from the aura of one street lamp to the next, obviously blinded by grief, unable to tell which way she was going. I cruised behind her until I saw her heavy body pitch forward onto a lawn and lie there, twitching. I stopped the car and got out. When I reached her she was pulling up grass with her hands and teeth and sobbing like an animal.

She made a retching sound as I helped her up. In the light from a nearby lamp, her dark eyes stared dazedly at me.

"No," she said. "No. No. No."

"Come on, Dorothy."

She started to fight me suddenly, whining, her lips wrenched back, saliva running between her clenched teeth and her jaw. I had to slap her before she went limp and allowed herself to be led to the car.

As I pulled away from the curb she started to cry again, shaking with deep sobs, her hands pressed across her face. At first I thought the noise she was making was only the sound of grief. Then I realized she was trying to talk—and, although I couldn't hear the words, I knew what it was she was saying.

"No, I'm not taking you to the police," I said. "And I'm not telling your father. But I'd get help, Dorothy. I mean it. And I don't want to see you in our neighborhood after tonight."

I was sorry I'd said the last but it came out automatically.

The rest of the way she sobbed and kept making those sounds of animal grief. I studiedly avoided her mind. When we reached her house, she pushed open the door and stumbled up the path. I pulled the door shut and made a fast U-turn. At that moment I didn't care what happened to her. I never wanted to see her again.

When I got home Anne was sitting on the living room sofa, still wearing her topcoat.

"Is he all right?" I asked.

"Yes. I took his things off. He's all right."

I noticed how pale her face was and realized that I hadn't been protecting her from anything; a woman has her own kind of knowing. I sat down next to her and put my arm around her.

"It's all over, Anne," I said.

It broke in her. She gasped and pressed her face against me. I felt her trembling.

"It's all right," I tried to comfort her.

After a while she calmed down and drew her head up. She looked at me with an expression I couldn't have fathomed just by looking at. Yet I knew what she was feeling—awe, withdrawal, anxiety.

"You knew, didn't you?" she said, quietly.

"Yes," I said, "I knew."

Her eyes shut. "Then it hasn't gone," she said. "It's still with us."

"Can you regret that now?" I asked. "If it had gone, we'd still be at The Lighthouse, thinking everything was—"

"Don't—" She pressed a hand over her eyes and began to cry softly. This time there was more relief than sorrow.

A broken laugh emptied from me unexpectedly. Anne looked up in disturbed surprise. "What is it?" she asked.

I shook my head and felt tears welling into my eyes.

" 'Real reliable,' " I said.

## TEN

THERE WAS NO DREAM THAT NIGHT. IT wasn't needed; Anne and I both knew that what Phil had started was still very much with us.

We spoke of it the next morning. Richard was still asleep. He'd woken up the night before when we'd taken off his pajamas again to reassure ourselves that nothing was wrong with him. He was making up for the lost sleep now. Anne and I sat drinking coffee in the kitchen before I went to work.

"Are you going to a doctor now?" she asked.

"Why?"

I saw how she attempted to hide the movement at her throat by sipping some coffee.

"Well . . . is it something you want?" she finally asked.

"It's not as if I asked for it," I said.

"That's not the point," she said.

"Well . . ." I stirred my coffee idly. "It's also not as if I were sick. You admit yourself it probably made all the difference last night."

She hesitated. Then she said, "Yes, I admit it. That doesn't change the rest of it, though."

"The rest?"

"You know what I mean."

I knew. It was with me even then; the taut pressuring at my skull, the queasy unsettledness in my stomach, the fearful memory of the woman, the dread of things unknown which might become known.

"All right, I know," I said. "I still can't believe it's a—a *harmful* faculty."

"What if you start reading my mind?" she asked. "You already have, a little. What if it becomes— wholesale?"

"I don't—"

"How would you like it if you were—*exposed* to me; naked to my mind?"

"Honey, I'm not trying to—to probe at you. You know that. The few little things I've picked up were inconsequential."

"Like last night?" she asked.

"We're talking about you, honey," I said.

"All right," she said and I sensed that she was almost nervous in my presence; it was a weird feeling. "All right. But if you can pick up those other things you can pick up what I think too."

I tried to joke but it was a mistake.

"What's the matter," I said, "do you have something to hide? Maybe a—"

"Everyone has something to hide!" she burst out. "And if they couldn't hide it, the world would be in a lot worse mess than it is."

At first I felt only stunned. I stared at her, taking the fallible course of wondering if there was something hidden behind her words. Then I knew that there wasn't, that she was right. Everyone has to have a secret place in his mind. Otherwise relationships would be impossible.

"All right," I said, "you're right. But I think I'd have to concentrate before I could—read your mind or anything."

"Did you concentrate on these other things?" she challenged.

"They were different. They were feelings, not—"

"Won't you admit anything?" she asked.

"Honey, this—power, whatever it is, may have saved our baby's life last night. I'm not anxious to kick it aside just like that."

"You'd rather torment me with it, is that it!"

"Torment you?"

She looked into her coffee and I could tell from the taut, fitful way in which she breathed how upset she was. I knew in other ways too.

"All right," she said. "All right."

"Oh . . . come on, Anne," I said. "Stop making me feel guilty for this thing. Is it my fault? It was your idiot brother who started it off."

I'd meant—with that unfortunate misconstruing of the male—that it should be a sort of joke. It didn't come out that way. Certainly she didn't take it that way.

She pretended not to take it at all. "Then you're not going to a doctor?"

"What in God's name could a doctor do?" I asked, angry at my own fallible defenses. "I'm not sick!"

Anne got up and put her cup and saucer in the sink. She stood looking out the window bleakly. He *is* sick. I knew that was what she was thinking.

"I'm not—sick," I said, adding the final word so she'd think I was just repeating myself, not answering her thought.

She turned to face me. Her expression was very grim.

"Tell me that tonight," she said, "when you wake up shuddering."

As I drove up to the house late that afternoon I saw Elsie watering her lawn. She was wearing tight yellow shorts and a yellow sweater several sizes too small for her.

As I got out of the Ford she was just setting down her sprinkler on the small, rectangular patch of grass between our driveways. She straightened up, put her hands on her hips and took a deep, calculating breath. Her sweater, had it been wood, would have creaked.

"There," she said. "That should do it."

"Without a doubt," I said, nodding, and pulled up the garage door. Already I felt that trickling of intrusion in my mind again. I pressed my teeth together and turned back to the car.

"Hey, what happened last night?" Elsie asked. "I called Dorothy today and her father said she's not baby-sitting any more. What'd you do—hypnotize her?" A twisted thread of thought from her mind told me what she half-imagined I'd done. I felt my stomach churning.

"You got me," I said, blandly. "Nothing happened."

"Oh?" She sounded disappointed.

I got into the car and drove it into the garage. As I got out and slammed the door I saw her standing out there, hands still pressed to her hips, shoulders designedly back, waiting. I started to walk toward the back garage door, then realized that would be too overt a rebuff and, with a sigh, I went back out the front way and reached up to lower the overhead door.

"I'm having some friends over tomorrow night,"

Elsie said. "Why don't you and Anne drop by? Might be fun."

"We'd like to, Elsie," I said, "but we're having dinner at her mother's house tomorrow night."

"Oh? That's a long drive." Anne's mother lived in Santa Barbara.

"I know," I said, mentally kicking myself for picking such a poor lie. The door banged down. "We don't see her very often, though." Oh, well, I thought, we can always eat out and go to a drive-in movie.

Elsie ran smoothing hands over her shorts.

"You sure you didn't hypnotize Dorothy and tell her not to sit for me any more?" she asked. There was a mince to her voice too; the kind she had in her walk.

"No, that's Phil's department," I said, turning away. "Say hello to Ron for me. Sorry about tomorrow night."

She didn't answer. She must have been aware of the fact that I was avoiding conversation. There was no help for that. I just couldn't take much exposure to her mind.

When I opened the front door, Richard came running out of the kitchen. "Daddy!" he cried.

As I swept my son into my arms I felt a burst of love from him. He kissed my cheek and tightened his small arms around my neck. Inchoate, wordless affection seemed to pour into me; love beyond words, beyond expression, a surging of trust and need and unquestioning devotion. Sometimes I think the whole experience—with all its hideous points—was worth it for that brief moment.

"Hello, baby," I murmured. "How are you?"

"Fi," he said. "How you?"

I pressed my face against his warm neck. Then Anne came out of the kitchen and the sensation dwindled. I walked over to her and kissed her. It wasn't returned.

"Hello," I said.

"Hello, Tom," she answered, quietly. That sense of withdrawal was still in her. I kissed her again and put my arm around her. She tried to smile but it was strained.

"I went to a doctor today," I said.

For a second there was a leaping of hope in her mind but then it funneled off. She looked at me bleakly. *And?* The word touched my mind.

"And?" she asked.

I swallowed, smiled. "Nothing," I said, trying to make it sound like consolation. "I'm in perfect physical shape."

"I see." Quiet; subdued.

"Honey, I did what you asked."

Her lips pressed together. "I'm sorry," she said, "I can't help it."

After she'd gone into the kitchen, I sat down with Richard for a few minutes and talked to him. Presently, I put him down and went to wash up for supper.

"The girl left her glasses here last night," was the first thing Anne said at supper.

"Oh? Well . . ." I made a disconcerted sound. "I really don't think I'd care to take them back. Maybe we can mail them."

"I threw them out," she said flatly and I felt a momentary burst of that protective hatred that had been in her the night before. I decided then that I'd have to concentrate on not anticipating her words. Her thoughts were coming too clearly now, too easily.

"Did you give Elizabeth her comb?" I asked.

Anne shook her head. "No. I forgot."

"Oh."

Silence a while. Then, as if it were the usual thing, I turned to Richard with a smile.

"Did you baby?" I asked. "What was she—"

Anne's fork crashed down on her plate.

*"Tom, he didn't say anything."* Her voice was so restrained it shook.

I stared at her a long time before looking down at my food.

"Mama?" Richard asked. "What, mama?"

"Eat your food, Richard," she said quietly.

We ate in silence for a few minutes.

"Oh, I . . . forgot to tell you," I said finally, "I'm not working tomorrow. I don't have to."

Anne picked up her coffee cup without looking at me.

"That's nice," she said.

I jolted up with a rasping cry, my body alive with apprehension.

Everything had suddenly been torn away; my life was only this moment of sudden waking and staring toward the living room where the woman was, waiting for me.

Then I became conscious of Anne awake, looking at me in the darkness. She didn't speak. She didn't make a sound; but I knew the angry fear in her.

Deliberately, ignoring every impulse screaming in my mind, I lay back and let breath trickle from my lungs, then lay there fighting the need to shiver violently. I clutched at the sheet with talonlike fingers and closed my eyes tightly. My brain seemed lightninged with awareness, my body tense and sick with it. But I had to pretend it was nothing. I knew she was there, waiting.

I don't know how long it was that I struggled against the pull of that woman. She was a living presence to me now. I actually hated her as I would hate another human being; hated her for being in there, for trying to drag me to herself with cords of icy demand.

Only after a long while did I sense a breaking up of her power. Still I remained tense, ready to fight. Only when it had passed completely did I let my muscles go limp. I lay there, strengthless, knowing that Anne was still awake.

I jolted again when the lamp clicked on.

For a moment she said nothing; just looked at me without expression. There the resistance in her seemed to drain off. She looked at me more carefully.

"You're soaking wet," she said.

I looked at her speechlessly, feeling the cold drops trickle down across my cheeks.

"Oh . . . Tom." She threw aside the covers and suddenly ran from the room. I heard her go into the bathroom, then she came back with a towel. Sitting quickly on the edge of the bed, she began patting my face. She didn't say anything.

When she'd finished, she put down the towel and brushed back my damp hair with her fingers.

"What am I doing to you?" she asked.

"What?"

"I should be helping you, not fighting you," she said.

I must have looked very frightened and very hapless because she leaned over and pressed her cheek against mine.

"Tom. Tom," she whispered, "I'm sorry, darling."

After a few moments she kissed my cheek and sat up. I could tell from the obdurate expression on her face that she was going to try to face it fully and resolutely.

"She—was in there again?" she asked.

"Yes."

"And . . . if you'd gone in," she said, "do you think you'd have seen her?"

I drew in a deep breath and let it flutter out.

"I don't know," I said. "I just don't know."

"You're sure she exists, though," she said, "I mean—"

"She exists." I knew she had been about to ask me if I was sure the woman didn't exist in my mind only. "I don't know who she is or what she wants here but . . . she exists." I swallowed. "Or *did*."

"You . . . really think she's a—"

I shook my head tiredly. "I don't know, Anne," I said. "It doesn't make sense. Why should a place like this be haunted? It's only a couple of years old—and the only person who ever lived here was Mrs. Sentas' sister. And she just went east." I smiled wryly at the memory. "Not west," I repeated Phil's little joke.

She had to smile.

"Tom, Tom," she said, "remind me to kick my baby brother right smack in the teeth the next time we see him."

"Will do," I said weakly.

She hesitated a moment, then said, "You think maybe we should—"

"No," I said, forgetting my resolve not to anticipate her words. "I don't think Phil could help. Although it wouldn't hurt to write him and tell him to cut out hypnotizing people if he doesn't know what he's doing."

"I'll write in the morning," she said.

In a little while, she turned off the lamp and lay down beside me.

"Do you forgive me?" she asked.

"Oh, honey . . ." I put my arms around her and felt the warm fullness of her body against me. "There's nothing to forgive."

Which was when it came to me; simply, with absolute clarity.

I started to tell her, then stopped.

"What were you going to say?" she asked.

I swallowed. "Uh . . . in order to get out of going to another of her damned parties," I said, "I told Elsie we were going to your mother's tomorrow night for dinner."

"Oh." Anne made an amused sound. "So what do we do? Take in a drive-in movie until it's safe to return?"

"Exactly."

I lay there quietly, holding her close. What I'd started to say to her hadn't been about Elsie. I'd only said that to conceal my original words. Because, as I'd started to speak them, it had occurred to me that Anne might not want to hear them; whether she believed them or not. And, somehow, I felt that she would believe them now—even though the working out of them might be only an accident. After all there was a fifty percent chance of my being right no matter how or why I made the prediction—that our coming baby would be a girl.

# ELEVEN

THE LETTER WAS DELIVERED SHORTLY after ten the next morning.

I took it into the kitchen to Anne, wondering why I felt so uneasy about it. I could see, from the handwriting on the envelope, that it was from her father. For a moment, I thought about my telling Elsie we were going to see Anne's mother that night; and wondered if it had been more than a coincidence.

Anne opened the letter and started to read it. I watched the expression of worry come into her face.

"Oh, no," she said.

It *is* your mother. I almost spoke the words aloud; then, quickly, closed my mouth before she noticed. She looked up.

"Mother's ill," she said.

I stared at her. I could hear the clock ticking on the cupboard.

"No," I said.

She thought I was referring to the letter. She went on reading it and I felt a great weight dragging down inside of me. I kept staring at Anne, beginning to feel sick.

"Dad say she's—"

She stopped instantly and looked at me in blank surprise.

She started to speak, stopped again. She did this several times. When, at last, she managed to force it, I knew it was against her will.

"What is it?" Her voice was low and frightened. I shook my head suddenly.

"Nothing," I said. My voice sounded brittle and artificial.

She kept looking at me. I felt my heart thudding heavily. I couldn't take my eyes from her. I saw her chest shake with uncontrolled breath.

"I want you to tell me what it is," she said.

"It's nothing." I felt dizzy. The room wavered around me. I thought I was going to fall.

"What *is* it?"

"It's nothing." Like a brainless parrot repeating. I kept staring at her.

"Tom—"

That was when the phone rang.

The sound that came from me was terrible. It was a moaning sound, a guttural, shaking exhalation of fright. Anne actually shrank back from me.

The phone kept ringing.

*"What is it?"* Her voice was hollow, ready to shatter.

I swallowed but the lump stayed in my throat. The phone kept ringing, ringing, I tried to speak but couldn't. I shook my head again. That's all I could do; shake my head.

Suddenly, with a gasp, she pushed by me and I stayed rooted there as she ran across the living room into the hall. The ringing stopped.

"Hello," I heard her say. Silence. *"Dad!"*

And that was all. Absolute silence. I pressed both shaking palms down on the sink counter and stood there staring at the spread fingers.

I heard her hang up. I stood waiting. Don't, I thought. Don't come in here. Don't look at me. I heard her footsteps, slow and heavy, moving across the living-room rug. Don't, I begged. Please. *Don't look at me.*

I heard her stop in the kitchen doorway. She didn't speak. I swallowed dryly. Then I had to turn. I couldn't bear it, just standing there with all her thoughts assailing me.

I turned.

She was staring at me. I'd seen a stare like that only once before in my lifetime. It was on the face of a little girl who was looking at her dog lying crushed in the street; a look compounded of speechless horror and complete, overwhelming disbelief.

"You knew," she said.

I reached out an imploring hand.

"You *knew*," she said—and there was no hiding the revulsion in her voice now; the fear. "You knew this too. You knew before he called."

"Anne—"

With a gagging sound, she whirled and fled the living room. I started after her. "Anne!"

She rushed into the bathroom and slammed the door behind her. I banged against it just after she'd locked it. Inside, I heard the start of her dry, chest-racking sobs.

"Anne, please!"

"Get away from me!" she cried. *"Get away from me!"*

I stood there, shaking helplessly, listening to her heartbroken sobs as she wept for her mother who had died that morning.

*   *   *

She left for Santa Barbara early that afternoon, taking
Richard with her. I didn't even ask if she wanted me
to go along. I knew she didn't. She hadn't spoken a
word to me from the time she'd come out of the bathroom till the time she drove away. Dry-eyed and still,
she'd packed a few of her and Richard's things into
an overnight bag, then dressed Richard and herself
and left. I didn't speak to her. Can you speak to your
wife at a time when you are a horror in her eyes?

After she'd gone, I stood on the lawn looking at the
spot where the car had turned left onto the boulevard.
The sun was hot on my back. It made my eyes water
the way it glinted metallically off the sidewalks. I stood
there a long time, motionless, feeling empty and dead.

"You too, haah?"

I twitched sharply as someone called to me. Looking across the street I saw Frank in his shorts coming
out of his garage with a lawn mower.

"I thought you were a staunch supporter of Saturday work," he called.

I stared at him. He put down the mower and
started toward me. With a convulsive shudder, I
turned away and went back into the house. As I closed
the door behind me, I saw him picking up the mower
again, squinting quizzically toward our house. He
shook his head and then bent over to adjust the grass-
catcher.

I turned from the door and walked to the sofa. I
sat down and lay my head back. I closed my eyes and
saw, in my mind, the look on her face when she had
come back from the telephone. And I remembered
something I'd said to Anne the night after Phil had
hypnotized me.

Maybe we're all monsters underneath, I'd said.

About two-thirty I got the lawn mower out of the
garage and started working on the front lawn. Staying

in the house was more than I could manage; it was a closet of cruel reminders. So I put on my shorts and tennis shoes and tried to forget by laboring.

It was a fruitless effort. The monotonous act of pushing the whirring mower back and forth across the grass, if anything, enhanced introspection. Then again, in the state I was in, I doubt if there was an activity in the world which could have made me forget.

To put it simply—life had become a nightmare.

Not even a week had passed since that party at Elsie's house; yet, in those short days, more incredible things had happened to me than had happened in the previous twenty-seven years. And it was getting worse; much worse. I dreaded the coming days.

I thought about Anne, about the horror in her eyes as she realized that I'd known her mother was dead—even before her father had phoned. I put myself in her position. It wasn't hard to see why she'd reacted as she had. The double shock of dread and grief could have snapped anyone.

"Hey, there."

I started and looked around. Harry Sentas was standing on his porch looking at me and I realized that I was halfway onto his lawn, cutting a crooked swath lower than the level of his grass.

"Oh, I—I'm sorry," I said, flustered. "I must have been dreaming."

He grunted and, as I turned with a nervous smile and started back again, I saw, from the corner of my eye, Sentas step down off his porch to examine the damage.

I kept mowing without looking up until he'd gone into his house again. Then I dropped the mower and went in for a towel. I sat on the edge of the cool cement porch, mopping at my face and staring across the street at Frank's house.

I thought about picking up his and Elizabeth's thoughts. I thought about his having an affair with a redhead at the plant. I thought about Elsie hiding the carnal clutter of her mind behind a face of bland innocence; about her brow-beating her husband mercilessly. I thought about Sentas and his wife and the tension that always seemed to be between them. I thought about the bus driver up the block who was an alcoholic who spent half his weekends in jail; about the housewife on the next street who slept with high school boys while her salesman husband was on the road. I thought about Anne and myself, about the incredible things that were happening to us.

All these things taking place in this peaceful neighborhood of quiet, little houses basking in the sun. I thought of that. It reminded me of Jekyll and Hyde. The neighborhood was two creatures. One presented a clean, smiling countenance to the world and, beneath, maintained quite another one. It was hideous, in a way, to consider the world of twists and warps that existed behind the pleasant setting of Tulley Street.

So hideous that I got up and started mowing again and tried to blank my mind.

It was about then, I think, that I considered the possibility that I was losing my mind. I mean *considered* it. Before that it had been a droll fancy to smile about. It was no longer that.

It was something I had to face. My mind was a prism. It broke up thought rays and scattered them into visions and impressions. That was simple enough. The difficult part lay in determining where those rays came from—without or *within*.

While I was finishing up the lawn, Ron came out of his house and got into their Pontiac convertible which was standing in the driveway. He made a little gesture of greeting with his hand and squeezed out a smile. I smiled back.

"May I borrow your edger?" I called.

He looked blank a moment, then nodded.

"Is it in the garage?" I asked.

"I think so."

After he'd driven off, I finished up the lawn, emptied the grass-catcher and put the mower back in the garage. Then I went into Elsie's garage (like the house it, too, seemed to belong only to Elsie). I looked around in the gloom but couldn't find the edger. I stopped for a few moments and thumbed through a magazine from the pile of true confessions and screen romances which were Elsie's only mental fare. Once, when she'd brought herself a small, wrought-iron bookcase, she'd come over and asked if she could borrow some books to display that night at a party— books with pretty jackets, she'd specified. She didn't notice that I'd slipped in *Ulysses* and *The Well of Loneliness*. For that matter, I doubt if any of her guests noticed either.

I tossed down the magazine, looked a little more for the edger, then went outside again. As I came out, Elsie was just closing the kitchen door.

"Hi," she said, brightly. "What are you doing in my garage?"

"Setting a fire," I said.

"Oh, yeah? You better not," she said. She was wearing that clinging bathing suit again. Her shoulders and upper chest were well tanned. She went to the beach three days a week with Candy.

"Do you want something?" she asked.

At first I was going to say no, then I decided I was being absurd about her. I told her I'd like to borrow the edger.

"Oh. Didn't you find it?" she asked as she came up to me. She looked up at me with those brown eyes that always seemed to be searching for something. *You're cute.* I felt the words stroke at my mind. I had the momentary urge to say, *No, I'm not* just to see what her reaction would be. It would have been, I'm sure, one of apparent surprise. She would have sworn on the Bible, of course, that she'd never thought any such thing.

"No, I don't think it's in there," I said.

"Sure it is. Come on. I'll show you."

I followed her into the dim, oily-smelling garage.

"I *know* it's in here somewhere," she said, hands on hips. She walked around the wall, looking behind the old blanket-covered refrigerator, the washing machine, the arm chair.

"*I* know," she said. She knelt on the old, sheet-covered sofa and looked behind it, the bathing suit growing drum-taut across her hips.

"There it is," she said. "Candy put it there the other day." She reached down and the bathing suit slipped a little, exposing the white tops of her breasts. She looked up at me as if she were concentrating on reaching the edger. I felt my stomach muscles tightening of their own accord. *Come to me.* The words seemed sharply distinct in my mind. They might have been spoken aloud. *Come to me, Tommy baby. I'll do something you'll like.*

I let out a shaking breath.

"Can't you reach it?" I asked.

It was a weird feeling to stand there play-acting, sensing the levels beneath this outwardly ordinary scene. To stand there talking casually when all the time I knew what she was thinking.

She slumped down on the sofa. "I can't," she said.

*You're lying,* I thought. I knew she could reach it. I didn't say anything. I started forward, robotlike. I knelt on the sofa and looked over the back. I saw the edger lying on the floor. With a grunt, I reached down. Elsie got on her knees again and I felt the warmth of her leg touch mine.

"Can you reach it?" she asked. I swallowed dryly. Her thoughts were like hands on my mind.

"I think so." I wanted to get up and walk out of there but I couldn't.

As a matter of fact, it was a little difficult to reach. I leaned over further. Elsie pressed closer. Now her side touched mine. It made my flesh crawl. I could smell the odor of her slightly sweaty body, of her hair. I could hear her breathing and feel the tickling drift of it across my shoulder and neck.

My hand closed over the edger.

"There," she said and her leg seemed to nudge me. Her cheek was almost against mine. "You've got it now," she said, *Tommy.* My breath caught as the sentence was finished in my mind.

I straightened up and turned to her. *Tommy?* It was a question now. As if she were speaking it in a low, husky voice. *Tommy?*

"Well . . ." I said.

I hesitated too long. I couldn't help it. Her thoughts seemed to thread themselves around me in great, tangling swirls. My heart was thudding like a slowly beaten tympani.

She seemed to lean forward. To this day I don't know if she really did or if I just imagined it. I felt dizzy. It could have happened either way.

"Anything else?" she asked.

*No!* The word scaled across my mind like a hand toppling the blocks of hungry thought she was building there. I drew back and saw how her breasts surged slowly against the binding of her suit as she drew in a deep breath.

"I don't think so," I said. I was startled at the strained sound of my voice.

"Sure now?" she asked. I felt her breath clouding

warmly across my face. I felt as I had when Phil's hypnosis had begun to work; devoured by an invisible, enervating force. I stood up limply.

"Yeah, I—think so," I said.

She stood too. She was close to me. I'm sure it was imagination but it seemed as if her body were radiating heat.

"All right then," she said.

The garage seemed to fall into place again. She was no longer a strength-draining incarnation of lust but only plump Elsie, our next-door neighbor, with a slightly silly smile on her face.

I turned for the door.

"If there's anything else," she said, "let me know."

"Okay," I said. I felt my legs shaking a little under me.

"Get back in the house, Candy," I heard Elsie say calmly as I moved down the alley.

I walked back to the house, left the edger on the porch and went in. I sank down on a chair and sat there weakly.

I felt like some sort of fantastic actor who could play two scenes simultaneously using not only the same setting but the same dialogue. That was the frightening thing about it. Anyone could have stood there and watched us and thought it innocuous; a pleasant summer's day flirtation which lasted a few moments, then ended. They wouldn't have seen the part of it that went on underneath.

I began to shake. Because, suddenly, I knew that Elsie's mind had so overwhelmed mine that my reaction had been one of shock and ineffectual defense. I had been vulnerable.

Which meant that I was a pawn. Up till that moment I had been under the somewhat comforting delusion that I had some power over this new capacity. Now it had become terribly clear that I didn't. It was not, as I had said to Anne, an increase. It was not a strength added to me; a strength which I could manipulate. It was as if a brainless monster had been set loose in my mind and was roaming, uncontrolled.

I was helpless.

# TWELVE

**N**IGHT.

I sat in the kitchen, drinking beer and staring at the tablecloth.

Hating Anne for leaving me alone.

"Why," I remember saying, as if she could hear me, "why didn't you let me go with you? Was it my fault I knew your mother was dead? Did I ask to know it? Was that enough reason to leave me here alone?"

I closed my eyes. I'd walked a mile and a half to a local movie just to get out of the house. I'd gone to a bar after that and had a few beers and watched the fights on television. I'd stopped at a liquor store on the way back and bought two quarts of beer and the Sunday papers. I'd read the papers through, glancing at everything, assimilating nothing. I'd finished one quart of beer, then been unable to see clearly enough to read. I'd watched television, staring glumly at a panel show, insulting the performers angrily. Finally,

I'd turned it off and stood there, staring at the contracting blob of gray light, watching the few remaining flickers before the tube grew black. Then I'd gone into the kitchen where I was now, sitting, working at the second quart of beer.

And waiting.

I knew there was no escaping. I couldn't sleep in the street. Sooner or later I had to lie down on the bed and go to sleep.

When I did, she'd return.

It was as much an assurance in my mind as it was an assurance that, after the funeral, Anne would come back with Richard.

"Too late," I berated her from eighty miles away. "Too late. You'll come back and it'll be too—"

I stiffened. Was that a sound in the living room? I bit my teeth together and listened so hard my eardrums hurt. I sat there frozenly, staring at the tablecloth, unable to look into the semi-lit living room.

"Are you in there?" I muttered. "Are you?"

I flung up my head suddenly.

"Well, *are* you!"

She wasn't. Something that sounded terribly like a sob broke in my chest. I heard it. I was afraid. I was a baby terrified of the dark, a little boy afraid of ghosts. All the years of reason and dogma had been stripped away. I'd been drinking beer in the hope of stultifying awareness. It had only increased it by lowering the barriers of conscious resistance. Don't ever get drunk if you want to avoid the tensions within; I found that out. Drinking only opens the gates and lets out the prisoners you can keep locked in with conscious will.

"I hate you," I said, drunkenly. "I hate you for leaving me. What kind of wife are you who'd leave me here alone? You know she's here. You know she wants me for something. You—"

I gasped as I heard a loud laughing in the next house. I heard Elsie saying brightly, "Oh, you *stop* that now!"

I shuddered. We are all monsters underneath, I thought.

"And the most monstrous of monsters is the female monster," I mumbled, "because they are shrewd monsters, because they are monsters of deceit, because they can lurk monstrously, hiding themselves behind a veneer of falsity, because they are monsters of deception."

I slumped forward, resting my head on my arms and wondered, for a moment, if I should go across the alley to Elsie's party. I knew I couldn't, though. To be exposed to her mind with all those people around; that was more than I could take.

"Anne, I don't want you to—"

I stopped. I stood dizzily and carried the beer bottle to the sink. I poured out the beer and watched its amber frothing as it disappeared down the drain. Then I put the bottle down.

Alone.

"I'm alone in this house."

I drove down a fist onto the sink counter. "Why'd you leave me alone?" I asked furiously.

I turned and walked weavingly to the kitchen doorway. Here, Anne had stood that very morning, staring at me in horror. I remembered that look. In detail.

"I asked for it, I suppose," I said. "I suppose I—"

My head snapped as I looked around the living room.

"All right, where are you?" I yelled. "God damn it, if—!"

I jolted as the phone rang. I stood rooted there, staring toward the hall.

Then, abruptly, I was running wildly across the rug, I was lurching into the hall, jerking up the receiver.

"Anne?"

"Tom. Where have you been? I've been calling all night."

I closed my eyes and felt the tension draining off.

"Tom?"

"I've been out," I said. "I . . . couldn't stay in the house. I went to a movie."

"You sound sick."

"It's nothing," I said. "I'm all right. I'm . . . just happy to hear from you."

"Tom. I . . . I don't know what to say. Except that—hearing about mother and then, on top of that . . ."

"I know, I know. You don't have to explain, darling," I said. "I understand perfectly. Just tell me you don't hate me, you don't—"

"Darling, what are you saying?" she asked. "Of course, I don't hate you. I was foolish and—"

"No, no, no. Don't blame yourself. It's all right. Believe me, it's all right. As long as I know you don't hate me."

"Oh . . . Tom. Darling."

"Are you all right? Is Richard all right?"

"Yes, of course, Tom. You sound so upset."

"Oh . . ." I laughed weakly. "It's just two quarts of beer talking. I've been consoling myself."

"Oh, darling, I'm so sorry," she said. "Please forgive me. I didn't mean what I said, you know I didn't mean what I—"

"It's all right, baby. It's all right." I swallowed. "When . . . when is the funeral?"

"Tomorrow afternoon," she said.

"Oh. How's your father?"

"He's . . . taking it very well." She paused. "I wish you were here with me. It was terrible of me to leave you like that."

"I wish I was there too. Shall I come up by bus?"

"Oh, no. I'll be home tomorrow evening. I don't want to ask you to—"

"I will, though. I will."

"No, darling. Just stay home. And . . . take it easy."

It was her last three words that did it.

I don't know what it was about the way she spoke them—but it made me stiffen defensively. And, as she went on, I began to realize that she was hiding something. By the time we said good night and she'd hung up, I felt almost as bad as I had before she'd called.

What was it? I stood there holding the receiver, listening to the thin buzzing in my ear.

As I put it down, it came to me.

She thought I was losing my mind.

I sat down heavily on the sofa and sat there trembling. I couldn't adjust to this, I just couldn't. Yes, I'd given it consideration myself but I didn't believe it. Anne did. So much so that she hadn't even told me she was thinking it. She'd humored me; patronized me.

My hands closed into fists.

"Speak gently to the foaming madman," I muttered tensely. "Talk to him in honeyed words lest he rise up and slay you. Oh . . . *God!*"

I drove down white-knuckled fists on my legs.

It was in that state of hurt and rage that I felt it start in me.

I'd sat there about an hour, I guess; head back, eyes staring at the ceiling.

Abruptly, I felt the tingling in my head.

I didn't fight it. Calmly, I decided that I wanted it to come. I felt a need to have it come. I even reached over casually and switched off the table lamp, then lay back in the darkness again and concentrated on making it come.

That seemed to impede it, so instead of trying to help it along, I relaxed and let it take its own course.

Never was I more aware that I was only a resourceless channel for its flow. But I didn't fight that. I was resentful; at Anne, at the world, it seemed, for doubting me. All right, if they wanted to think that I was losing my sanity, let them.

Anger made it fade too. Any conscious flare of volition seemed to limit its ascent. Again I relaxed. I lay back, waiting, not caring. I realized that the reason it had taken so long that first night was that I had been opposing it, albeit without direction.

It was very much as it had been that first night—but greatly accelerated. There were the flashings and sparks of emotion and thought. There were the visions and the burning interweave of memories, the faces rushing by, the ideas, the conceptions—all like shooting stars across a black firmament of half-drugged observation.

Then it all seemed to reach its zenith again and I realized that, rather than disappearing, it hovered at that peak, holding me in a vise of taut awareness.

*Now.*

Slowly, as if Anne had just come into the room and I were raising my head to look at her, I looked toward the window.

A dream? No dream ever had such stark reality to it. I could almost *feel* the smooth, white flesh of her, the texture of her black-patterned dress, the tangled softness of her hair. I felt a grim satisfaction seeing her there; as if she had come to prove me, to disprove others. And I realized that the reason I hadn't seen her that other night was that Anne's presence had weakened the woman's influence.

Then the piercing look of those dark eyes began to weaken satisfaction and a chill of fright began to creep along my limbs. I sat there rigidly and I could even hear the sounds of Elsie's party next door.

"Who are you?" I asked. My voice was almost a whisper.

No answer. I felt a cold prickling sensation along my scalp.

"What do you want?"

No answer. I stared at her. I ran my eyes over her, taking in every detail; the odd dress, the pearls, the watch on her left wrist, the pearl ring on the third finger of her left hand, the dark suede shoes, the stockings, even the fullness of her figure. She stood without moving as I looked at her.

"What do you want?" I asked again.

Her eyes pleaded again. I saw her white lips stir. And, suddenly, I was leaning forward, my heart pounding.

"Tell me," I said, suddenly anxious, realizing she wouldn't stay much longer. "*Tell* me. *Please.*"

But I was talking to a dark and empty living room. I stared at where she'd been. Nothing.

Except for one thing.

A faint, pathetic sobbing in the darkness.

Gone in an instant.

I was going to ask Mrs. Sentas what her sister looked like before I realized that it was rather a strange question for me to be asking. What was I supposed to tell her when she asked why I wanted to know? *Well, you see, I keep seeing this ghost in my living room and . . .*

Thirty days, next case, as they say.

By then, as a matter of fact, I no longer thought of the woman as being a ghost. My mind shrank now from bridging that chasm again. Remembering the emotion that had filled me when I'd believed I'd found proof of what men call "the beyond"—I rejected re-involvement in such belief. I retained, at least, that much skepticism. I no longer doubted the woman's existence at all. That was acceptance enough for then, considering what it implied.

I woke up about nine the next morning—Sunday— and lay there quietly looking at the patterns of sunlight on the ceiling. For a few moments the inevitable rise of disbelief came again. It faded quickly. I could not doubt now. Even if there were not the ever-present headache and nagging stomach tension, I would have had to believe.

And it was very strange to lie there and know that everything that had happened to me had a measure of objectivity; that I wasn't losing my mind. Yet here I was in this sunlit bedroom and, across the street, I heard someone mowing his lawn. And, on the next street, some boy was working on his model airplane, the air rent faintly by the shrill buzz of the engine. And the sun was shining and people were going to church. And, through it all, I knew that these evidences of what we call "life" were only a scant portion of the over-all. I knew it. All doubts were gone now.

This is quite an acceptance.

After breakfast, after rejecting the idea of asking Mrs. Sentas, I went across the street to Frank and Elizabeth's house.

Elizabeth was sitting at the kitchen table drinking coffee as I came up on the back porch. I knocked softly and she looked up. A faint smile eased her features.

"Come in, Tom," she said.

I did.

"Good morning," I said.

"Good morning."

"The loafer still in bed?"

She nodded. "How's Anne?" she asked. "I didn't see her around yesterday."

I told her about Anne's mother.

"Oh, no," Elizabeth said, dismayed. "How terrible

for her." I sensed that she wanted to ask me why I hadn't gone to Santa Barbara too but felt it too undiplomatic a question.

"So you're all alone," she said. "Frank said he spoke to you yesterday and you . . ." Her voice trailed off.

"I didn't hear him," I said. "I guess I was in a fog."

"I told him you probably hadn't heard him," she said. She smiled. "Would you like some coffee?"

"Yes. Thank you." Drinking coffee with her would give me a chance to ask about Helen Driscoll.

Which I did after she'd poured me a cup of coffee and sat down again.

"What did she look like?" Elizabeth asked.

"Yes."

She deliberated. *Why do you want to know?* The gist of those words occurred to me and I knew she thought them. I almost answered before I stopped myself.

"Well, was she—?" I stopped again. I didn't want to feed a description to her.

"What were you going to say?" she asked.

"Nothing."

"Oh." Her eyes held on mine a moment and I thought how pretty she could be if there were only a little color, a little animation in her face—which is to say, a little happiness.

"I didn't really see much of her," she said. "We—we only moved in about six months before she left and—we never had anything to do with her. She kept to her—herself pretty much."

"I see."

"As to what she looked like," Elizabeth bit her lower lip contemplatively, "oh, she was—sort of tall. Dark hair. Dark eyes."

I found myself leaning forward, staring at her.

"Did she have a—sort of dark dress too?" I asked, trying—ineffectually, I'm afraid—to sound casual.

Elizabeth stared at me and her mind was a mixture of suspicion and curiosity.

"Dark dress?" she asked.

"Yes. Black with a—sort of—sort of pattern on it?"

"Well." She swallowed. "She had a dress she'd gotten in Tijuana," she said. "I saw one like it when Frank and I drove down there once."

"It was dark?"

"Yes," she said. "It was black. And it had little patterns on it. Like—Aztec symbols I guess they were."

*"And she wore it with a string of pearls?"*

She seemed to shrink back a little. I must have looked somewhat maniacal. I could barely hear her voice when she answered.

"Yes, she did," she said.

# THIRTEEN

I LEANED BACK, MY HANDS TREMBLING ON my lap.

"I guess you're wondering why I asked," I said, trying to keep the excitement from my voice.

"Well, I—" She seemed a little frightened of me.

"I found a small photograph in one of the cupboards over at the house," I said, "and I was just wondering if it was our previous tenant."

*"Oh."* I think she believed me. At any rate, the aura of suspiciousness seemed to fade from her mind.

I finished my coffee, managing to talk about the neighborhood in general terms. Then, as I got up, Elizabeth asked about her comb.

"Oh . . . good lord," I said, "do we still have it?"

She smiled. "It doesn't matter."

"I'll go get it right now."

"Oh, no, I can—"

"No, by God, I'm going to get it right now," I said.

"You've waited long enough." I opened the door. "I'll be right back."

"All right then."

As the door closed behind me, all the excitement flooded out; my fists clamped shut, breath shook in me. It *was* Helen Driscoll! That may have not proved life after death but it proved something just as exciting to me; that Helen Driscoll still wanted to be in that house and that, from a distance of three thousand miles, was transmitting that desire so strongly that I was actually *seeing* her in the living room.

I wished that Anne were back so I could tell her; so she could see what it was and stop worrying about my sanity. I no longer resented her attitude; it was natural under the circumstances. But those circumstances were far beyond what she imagined. For a few moments I had the premonition that she might not believe me. Then I realized that she must. Elizabeth was my witness. I'd never seen Helen Driscoll in my life.

Yet I'd asked about that dress and been right.

I was thinking about that as I came into the kitchen. The comb was on the window sill over the sink. I walked over and picked it up.

*"Uh!"*

My cry was short and breathless; the cry of a man who has touched something alive when he least expects it.

For, as my hand had closed over the comb, I'd felt a sudden, jagged tingle in my fingers; as if I'd touched an open wire. I'd recoiled and the comb had dropped into the sink.

I stood there shivering, staring down dumbly at the comb. I don't know what expression I had on my face but it must have been one of awed stupefaction. Stupefied was how I felt; and awed by dread that had been too quick to identify, yet too powerful to miss.

I reached down gingerly, then drew back my fingers as if the comb were something lethal. I swallowed dryly and kept staring at it, all thoughts of Helen Driscoll vanished. A new element had entered my mind, brushing everything away but itself.

I stood there about two minutes, staring, my mind stumbling over itself in an attempt to wrench reason from the situation. It couldn't. Imagine coming from your house one morning on the way to work, turning a corner and finding yourself confronted by a seven-headed dragon. Imagine your attempt to rationalize, to adjust, even to understand basically what it was you were looking at and realize at the same time that it was still you, going to work on an ordinary morning.

There are no established channels of acceptance in the mind for a sudden appearance of the bizarre. Which was why I stared and couldn't move; why I reached down to touch the comb at least a dozen times, then didn't touch. Why my mind seemed wooden and incapable.

Finally, I got a knife out of the cupboard drawer and reached down into the sink. I nudged the comb with it. Nothing. I touched it again. I felt nothing. I squinted at the comb and couldn't understand.

Then I put down the knife and picked up the comb again.

It was not so violent this time but it was still there. As I stood, stricken with helpless alarm, the room seemed to blacken and a coldness pressed at me.

*Death.* The concept was unmistakable.

I dropped the comb again and stood there shivering, looking down at it as it lay on the linoleum, looking quite harmless.

I couldn't stop trembling. Once again I was terribly aware of the uncertainty, the uncontrollability of my perception. It came always when I was far from expecting it. I recalled the experiment psychologists use to drive dogs insane. Whenever the dog leasts expects it—usually as it is bending over its bowl to eat—they strike a great pipe and the high, vibrating tones unnerve the dog. By the time this act has been repeated a few dozen times, the dog has gone mad and has degenerated into a twitching, slavering hulk of its former self, incapable of the slightest reasoning.

I felt this now; with the terrible added dimension that I could see it happening. I knew that, every once in a while, when I was not prepared for it, when I was emotionally off balance, these things would occur—jarring me badly. If it went on long enough, I too could be reduced to a pitiful creature of twitchings and apprehensions.

In a while, I put the comb in an envelope and took it back to Elizabeth.

It wasn't until I came into the kitchen and handed it to her that the awful connection occurred to me.

When the word *Death* had branded itself so unmistakably on my mind—*it was her comb in my hand.*

The day was an agony.

My exultation at having discovered who the woman was had been short-lived. I sat in the living room most of the day, *waiting* for something else to happen. That it didn't helped not at all. It isn't the shocks which can undo a man so much as not knowing when the shocks are coming.

By late afternoon, I was nerve-racked. A child's shout in the street made my muscles go spastic. The sound of a car horn made me jolt with a sucked-in gasp. The rattle of a breeze-stirred blind made me turn my head so quickly that needles of pain exploded in my neck. And, when the phone rang about five, the cup of coffee I was drinking jerked out of my hand as though endowed with sudden life and rolled across the living-room rug, spewing its brown contents.

I stood, trembling, and answered the phone. It was Anne. She told me that the funeral was over and she was going back to her father's house now to see some relatives. She'd start home about eight. I said fine.

"Are you all right?" she asked.

"Yes," I said, "I'm fine."

After I'd hung up, I gave up coffee and started on beer, hoping to relax the rubber-band tautness of my nerves. Anne was right, I thought as I picked up the pieces of broken cup and wiped up the coffee. She was right; I should go see Alan Porter. I probably will, too, I thought. Some time in the next week. Although, it occurred to me, how could he help? I knew by then that I wasn't insane but undirectedly receptive. What could he do to ameliorate that? I was a wireless set open to all bands, my controller gone. No sure hand rested on the knobs, no observing eye saw when messages were coming in and warned me ahead of time. It was all blind; and, because blind, terrifying.

As a matter of fact I got halfway through dialing Alan's home number before I hung up. No, I thought, he can't do anything. He deals with mental aberration. This is not what he deals with.

For some reason—whether it was the weather or me—what had been a hot day turned into a chilly evening. As it started to get dark, I put on a sweater but it did no good. Finally I decided to light a fire.

I got some pressed logs from a kitchen cupboard and put them on the grate, then cut off enough shavings to ignite them. It was about eight, I guess, when I lit the fire. Outside, it was just getting dark, the sun-reddened clouds beginning to purple in the sky.

I sat on the sofa, staring at the low flames and thinking about Elizabeth.

I tried to tell myself that it had been imagination, but that sort of defense was no longer of any use. I knew it wasn't imagination. Too many things had come true for me to doubt. I was afraid of this rude, misshapen power in me but I couldn't refute its existence.

But Elizabeth . . . poor, quiet Elizabeth. How could I just sit here thinking what I did? I knew then the curse of the prophet, the agony of the seen. How, I thought, could someone like Nostradamus stand the crushing horror of believing that he knew, step by awful step, the centuries ahead?

But how could she die? I wondered that.

The answer came almost simultaneous with the question. *In childbirth.* She was thin, with a narrow pelvis. And she'd never had a child. For all I knew, there was a history of unsuccessful pregnancies in her family.

I bit my lip and felt miserable thinking about it. What was it Anne had said? *All she wants is a baby.* It was so terribly true. It was what kept her going. I was sure of that. It was what made her able to stand all of Frank's cruel abuses; his tantrums and neglect.

And she would die, having never known her child.

I sat in that small, quiet living room, staring at the fire through a gelatinous haze of tears, crying for Elizabeth and for myself because we both needed help and there was no one to help.

Then, as I sat there, the fire began to fade and the room to darken. I got up and went over to prod the logs. I knelt before the fireplace and pulled the drawstrings for the chain screen. It whispered apart and I reached for the poker.

Again!

This time it was a cry of agony that tore back my lips. The poker flew from my hand and bounced darkly across the rug.

"No!" I remember sobbing, "No, no, no, no!" I felt almost deranged with fury and horror. I wanted to crawl into a shell and be rid of the world which was a forest of traps. Everywhere I turned there was menace, everything I touched could be imbued with a terrible life.

It was a long time before I could even stand. I huddled close to the floor, my head almost between my legs, my body shaking endlessly, a foaming nausea in my stomach. I kept gasping and gagging as if I were going to throw up. Even that would have been a relieving completion. As it was there was only time stopped and me frozen with it, alone and helpless and sick.

Finally, after hours, it seemed, it passed. I struggled shakily to my feet and lurched to the sofa. I fell down on it and turned on one lamp, another lamp. The fire had gone out. I stared at it a moment, then my eyes moved, as if drawn, to the poker. It was made of iron, painted black. A machine or man had twisted its end into a right angle. There was a coil-like handle on it. And that was all it was—a simple, functional object, without menace to the eye. Yet, to me, that poker possessed all the elements of nightmare—and I could no more have touched it again than I could have flown.

I was in the kitchen when Anne got home.

I'd been there for two hours, afraid to enter the living room even though I'd turned on every lamp. I'd sat there drinking beer and staring fixedly at the same pages of the Sunday comics, getting not one gleam of meaning from it, much less humor.

When she came in, I gasped involuntarily, my head flung up. I must have looked terrified. Unfortunately, she saw that expression before it was replaced by one of welcome.

She felt too, I'm certain, the tremble of me as I put my arms around her and kissed her.

"Hello, sweetheart," she said, gently.

"I'm glad you're back," I said; and my voice too; it gave me away it labored so.

I took in a long, wavering breath and smiled at her. "Where's Richard?" I asked.

She gestured toward the door with her head.

"Asleep in the back seat," she said. "I didn't want to lift him. My condition, you know."

"Of course." I smiled nervously. "I'll go get him."

"All right."

I was almost glad to get away from her eyes. I went outside and opened the back door of the Ford. Richard was warm and pink-cheeked, only his face visible under the blanket. For a moment I stood there looking at him, feeling a rush of love for him. I bent over and kissed his cheek. He sighed and his small hand stirred on the blanket.

"Oh, God, I love you, baby," I remember whispering to him. As if I were a doomed man taking a final look at his adored son.

As I went back into the house, carrying him, I saw Anne standing near the fireplace, the poker in her hands. She looked up at me. Her smile was strained.

"What happened?" she asked, trying to sound casual.

I swallowed. "I—had a fire," I said. "I dropped the poker and—didn't bother picking it up. Oh, and that spot is some coffee I spilled."

"Oh." She put the poker back in the rack as I started out of the room. I felt the nervous distrust in her mind as in her voice.

When I came back in she was sitting on the sofa. She smiled at me and patted the cushion next to her.

"Come sit by mama," she said.

I felt myself tense. I knew exactly what she felt and knew I couldn't tell her anything—about Helen Driscoll or Elizabeth or Elsie or the poker or anything.

I sat down beside her; and, even though I felt the

wall between us, it was still comforting to have her back; her love, her warmth, her restoring normality.

"Tell me about the . . ." I started, hoping to avoid discussion about myself.

"It was the usual thing," she said. I saw now that she'd been crying a lot. The flesh around her eyes was puffy. I put my arm around her neck and she leaned against me. For a moment our roles were reversed; I became the comforter.

"Was it terrible?" I asked.

She swallowed. "Pretty bad," she said. "Especially afterward. All the relatives together. Some people are so—so damned *jolly* after funerals."

"I know," I told her, "I know. It's a reaction."

We sat in silence a moment.

"How's your father?" I asked then.

"He's all right. He's . . . going to stay with my Uncle John for a month or so. They're going on a fishing trip in a few weeks, I think."

"Oh. That'll be . . . nice," I said. The word, like our conversation, was weak and avoiding the issue.

Silence again. I didn't attempt to break it. I knew that, sooner or later, I'd have to discuss it with her.

"Tom," she said, finally.

"Yes?"

I felt what she was going through; the dread, the fear of angering me, of hurting me with the wrong words. I realized that I had to help her.

"You're worried about my sanity, aren't you?" I said.

She started in my arms. I heard her swallow.

"That's . . . putting it rather—harshly," she said.

"Why put it politely?" I asked. I pressed my lips together in self-anger as I realized that already I was speaking coldly to her.

"Tom, I—"

"It's all right," I said. "I knew you felt this way last

night. I guess I've been stewing a little. But I'm not angry now. I . . . suppose it was inevitable you should feel this way."

For a moment I thought of using Helen Driscoll as evidence in my behalf but then realized it was too thin a verification. I decided that bringing her up now would only make things worse.

"What do you want me to do?" I asked. "Before you tell me, though, I want to let you know that I haven't the remotest doubt of my sanity. I know this is—supposedly—one of the sure signs of madness but—well, that's it. As far as I'm concerned I'm as sane as you are. I have—an *ability* which got started somehow. I—"

I stopped, knowing that if I went on I would begin to cite examples; in which case what had happened that day and the day before would slip out. I didn't want it to—not when she felt as she did.

"Well, you don't leave me much to say," she said. I could tell how unhappy she was with her situation.

"I don't know what *I* can say," I said.

I heard her swallow.

"Tom . . ." She drew in a quick breath. "Tom, when I came in tonight you looked at me as if—"

"I know, I know," I broke in. "I've been nervous, that's all. Maybe overwork."

"No, it's more than that," she said. "The dreams, what happened the other night with the sitter, the—the poker tonight. I don't know why you didn't pick it up but . . . it wasn't just because you didn't want to."

"Of course it was," I said. I'm not a good liar.

She seemed to hesitate.

"Will—you do something for me?" she asked.

"What?"

"Promise me you'll do it."

"Honey, I have to know what it—"

"All right, all right," she interrupted. "Will you write to your family and—"

"—and ask them if there are any nuts in the family?"

I tried to sound amused but succeeded only in sounding pettish.

"Tom, don't put it that way. I didn't start all this. Can't you understand? I'm carrying our child and it's hard enough as it is. I—I just can't take all this. Not without some attempt to understand."

"All right," I said. "All right. I'm sorry."

"You . . . *did* tell me about your father once," she said, "how he used to—you know, do . . . parlor tricks."

I looked at her in surprise.

"That's all they were," I said, "parlor tricks."

My answer, though, was purely automatic. Suddenly I was thinking that maybe it had a connection; a very definite connection.

While we sat there, I thought about how my father used to go out of the living room and ask one of us to pick out a name and phone number in the directory, any name, any number, anywhere in the whole, thick book. We'd do this and shut the book. Father would come in and open the directory and find the very name that had been chosen. It always used to be amusing and mystifying to us but, because father had been so casual about it, we'd never assumed for a second that it was anything more than a trick.

Now I wondered. And the word *heredity* was not the least word in my thoughts.

"*Will* you write to them?" Anne asked, breaking into my reflection.

"Oh. Yes . . . all right. I'll write them. Maybe I had a grandfather who was a medium or something, huh?"

"Tom, don't joke about it."

I patted her shoulder. "All right."

Later, while I was brushing my teeth, I heard Anne in the kitchen washing up the dishes. When she came into the bedroom she said, "Did you take back Elizabeth's comb?"

I sat down on the bed and bent over my shoes so she wouldn't see the expression on my face.

"Yes," I said, "this morning."

"Oh, good," said my wife.

# FOURTEEN

ANNE TOLD ME TO GO NEXT DOOR AND get back some piepans Elsie had borrowed. I said all right and I walked across the living room, stepping over the poker which was lying on the rug and went outside. Elizabeth was across the street lying on the grass. Doctors were bending over her. I felt very bad about it but I couldn't stop because Anne was anxious to get those piepans.

I went up the alley to Elsie's back porch. There was a sign on the door that read *Elsie's House*. I knocked and she opened the door. She was wearing a wet yellow housecoat that clung to her body. Come in, she said. I asked her if I could get the piepans. She said yes and she stooped down to get them out of the cupboard. The skirt of her housecoat slipped off her right leg and she looked up at me, smiling. Tommy? she asked. I backed away. She stood up with the piepans and brought them over to me. She handed them to me and they gave me an electric shock. I couldn't move and she began running her fingers through my hair. Tommy, she said, Tommy. The front of her housecoat came apart. She was naked underneath. Tommy, she begged, *Tommy*.

I tore away from her and pulled open the door. It stuck. She caught at my arm. Come to me, Tommy, she said. She pressed her body against me and started kissing my cheek. I jerked the door open and pulled away. Anne was standing on our back porch looking at us. Elsie giggled and said, Now you *stop* that, Tommy! Anne, for God's sake, I yelled, can't you see that it's her doing, not mine? Anne recoiled. She backed toward the kitchen door. Anne! I shouted. Get away from me! she cried.

I turned and struck Elsie in the face and, with a gasp, she fell back on the kitchen floor, white limbs thrashing. I'll kill you! she yelled. I whirled and ran down the alley. I turned left at the street and started running toward the boulevard. Dorothy passed me and I asked her where she thought she was going. To sit for Elsie, she said sullenly. Just stay away from *our* house, I told her. You go to hell, she said.

I kept running. Across the street I saw Frank pull up in his car and help out a little redhead. Just taking the boss home to dinner, he called to me with a grin. You animal! I shouted back. He snickered. He and the redhead walked past Elizabeth who was writhing on the grass, screaming with pain.

Now I was running and running. The houses rushed past me. At the boulevard I came to railroad tracks. That's funny, I thought, I never knew there were railroad tracks here. I started running along them, gasping for breath. Far ahead I saw spotlights glaring in the night like novas. I wonder what that is, I thought. I ran faster. I realized that I'd lost the pie-pans and Anne would be angry. Then I remembered

Elsie and knew that Anne wasn't going to talk to me anyway.

I kept running. I wonder what this is up here, I thought. Certainly looks like a lot of activity. Lights, men working and rushing around, sirens sounding.

Suddenly I stopped in my tracks, aghast. I stared at the awful scene. I was surrounded by it. There was a train but it was a vast tangle of wreckage. I saw the locomotive lying on its side, wheels still turning slowly, steam hissing from its funnel like the breath of a dying animal congealing in icy night air. I couldn't move. I stared at the scene. There were stretcher-bearers racing back and forth between ambulances and the bodies strewn about. I saw a head lying on some gravel. Just a head. I couldn't take my eyes off it.

One side, please, I heard a voice telling me. I turned and a policeman was leading some doctors past. My God, what happened? I asked him. Train derailed, he said.

I looked at the wreckage again. I could see how it had happened now. The locomotive had struck some object on the track and lurched over the tracks, gouged its juggernaut way through about twenty yards of earth before pitching over on its right side and flinging over the rest of the attached cars, then raked them, screeching and bouncing over the gravel-spread dirt until its own weight had stopped it suddenly and the lighter cars behind, still moving by their own inertia, had telescoped into a jagged, murderous heap.

Oh, no, I said. Oh, God, no.

I sat up. The darkness pressed coldly at my eyes. I heard Anne beside me, breathing heavily in her sleep.

I don't know why I did it; except that the dream still clung so strongly to my mind. I got up and stumbled into the kitchen. I switched on the light and pulled open a cupboard drawer. I took out Anne's grocery pad and pencil and took them over to the table. I sat down and wrote down every detail of my dream as I recalled it. It took up one and a half pages of short, chopped-off sentences like—*Train derailed. Ploughed through gravel. Turned on side. People fell from windows. Crushed underneath.*

It took me about five minutes to scrawl it all down. When I was finished I sat there limply, staring at what I'd written. Then I put down the pencil and stood, walked back to the bedroom not even wondering why I didn't see Helen Driscoll. I crawled back into bed with Anne and closed my eyes. For a moment I wonder why I'd dreamed what I had; why I'd bothered to write it down. I fell asleep without the answer.

The alarm clock buzzed at six-forty the next morning.

I opened my eyes and winced. My head was throbbing, my stomach twisted in knots. I groaned.

Anne pushed in the clock stop and turned back to me.

"What's the matter?" she asked.

"I don't feel so good," I said. The pain came in waves in my head. I had to brace myself to meet them. I had to lie motionless. Even when Anne shifted her weight on the mattress, it sent extra twinges of pain through my head.

"What is it?" she asked.

"Stomachache," I said. "Headache."

"The same thing," she said, looking at me concernedly. I didn't reply. I kept my eyes closed.

"Do you . . . want me to call a doctor?" she asked.

"No. No. I'll be all right. Just . . . phone the plant and tell them I can't make it to—" I gasped as a cramp hit my stomach. I turned on my side and drew up my legs.

"Honey, are you all right?"

The cramp eased. "I'm all right," I muttered. "I'll . . . just stay in bed a while."

"I'll call the plant."

I turned on my back as she went into the hall to phone. I stared at the ceiling thinking that it wasn't only the shocks and the waiting for them that could undo me. It was also the increasingly violent after-effects. I felt ill and depleted; as if some invisible vampire had sucked at my throat all night, draining away blood and life.

"I . . . don't suppose you want any breakfast," Anne said. She was back in the doorway.

"No. Thank you."

She came over and sat down beside me. She began to stroke my hair but even that slight pressure of her fingers increased the pain. Her hand twitched away.

"I'm sorry," she said.

"It's all right."

She swallowed. "Shall I—get you an aspirin?" she asked.

"I can try one," I said. I knew it was rest I needed, though.

"Tom, did you . . ." she began, then faltered and stopped. I knew she was thinking that I'd seen the woman again while she slept and it had, somehow, caused this.

"No," I said, "I didn't see her." I didn't even bother waiting for her to finish her sentence. Why hide it now? I thought.

"I see."

She sat there a moment longer as if she wanted to ask me questions. Then she got up and brought me an aspirin. She left me alone, closing the door softly behind her.

I lay there trying to sleep but unable to, listening to her and Richard in the next bedroom. Once, the door opened and Richard started in with a cheery,

"*Hi,* daddy!" but Anne drew him back, saying, "No, no, baby. Daddy doesn't feel good."

"He don fee goo?" Richard was asking as the door shut. I smiled to myself even though it hurt. I had to keep my face immobile for the pain to stay down.

I tried to sleep but I couldn't. I kept telling myself that something had to be done. Anne was right. I had to do *something.* There must be an answer. Maybe my friend Alan Porter *could* help. I didn't see how but— well, I couldn't go on like this indefinitely. The drawbacks were starting to outweigh the dubious advantages of this thing.

It was about ten minutes after she'd left that Anne returned.

She looked white.

She stood by the bed looking down at me fixedly. It was the same look she'd given me the morning her mother died.

I started to ask what it was, then stopped. There was no bridge needed; suddenly, no need for explanations. I had only to see that look on her face—and the grocery pad in her hand.

"You . . . heard it on the radio," I said, hollowly.

She couldn't speak.

"Did you?" I raised up on an elbow and winced at the pain. She stared at me. "Anne, *did* you?"

She nodded. Slowly.

"Oh, my God." I sank back on the pillow weakly and looked up at her, my chest rising and falling in fitful little movements. "Wh-when did it happen?"

"Last night," she said.

"Oh." It was all I could say.

"When did you write this thing?" she asked, quietly.

"Last night," I told her. "I . . . I dreamed it. Then I— woke up and wrote it down. I don't know why. I—"

She sank down slowly on the bed, looking dazed.

She glanced down at the pad, then at me. Her lips stirred soundlessly. She couldn't seem to find the right words.

"Maybe you'll believe me now," I remember saying.

She drew in a shaky breath.

"I don't know," she murmured. She looked down at the pad. "This," she said, "this."

We sat there silently, Anne staring at the pad, me staring at her. There was nothing to say. It was all there on the surface where it could be easily seen.

In a short while she got up and walked out of the room. I heard her go out of the house. A few minutes later she was back. She came into the bedroom again. She'd gone next door to borrow Elsie's *Mirror-News*.

We spent the next half hour matching up what I'd written with what was in the paper.

*Train derailed*, I'd written. "According to the fireman, Maxwell Taylor," the paper wrote, "there was an obstruction in their path which caused the locomotive to leap the tracks."

*Spotlights. Ambulances. Stretcher-bearers*, I'd written. The paper reported: "The scene was a nightmare under glaring spotlights as stretcher-bearers raced back and forth between their ambulances and the victims who were strewn across an area of a hundred square yards."

*Head on ground*, I'd written. Columnist Paul Coates had written: "I saw a head lying on the ground. Just a head. An intern got a blanket and covered it."

I slumped back on the pillow and looked at Anne. My hands stirred feebly on the bedclothes.

She shook her head.

"I . . . I don't know," she said. "I just don't know what to say." She looked at page one of the paper, at the glaring, horrific headline: TRAIN WRECK

KILLS 47. At the picture which I might have taken in my dream.

"I don't know," she said. "I just don't know."

I slept most of the day; a heavy, drugged sleep, my body building up the energy that had been drawn from me.

I woke about three and dressed. Anne was in the kitchen, shelling peas. As I crossed the living room I saw Richard and Candy in the back yard. They had found a kitten and were shrieking with delight as it chased its tail. I smiled weakly and went into the kitchen.

Anne looked up from the table. I sat down across from her.

"Feel better?" she asked.

"Yes."

"Good. Are you hungry?"

"Not much. I'd like some coffee, though."

She got it for me. I sat sipping it while she went on with her shelling.

"Have you—told anyone?" I asked.

She made a sound which to anyone else but me would have sounded like a sound of amusement.

"Who would I tell?" she asked. "Elsie? Elizabeth?"

"I don't know."

"I have no intention of telling anyone," she said.

"No," I said, "of course not."

She put down her knife. "Tom," she said firmly.

"What?"

"What else has happened?"

"What else?"

"While I was in Santa Barbara," she said, "and before that." She saw the look on my face and added, "I won't say a word, Tom. I . . . have to believe you. After what happened this morning."

"You mean you don't think I'm—"

"How can I now?" she said.

So I told her—about Helen Driscoll, about Elizabeth's comb, about the poker, about Elsie (but not about the dream). It was all told in a very short time.

When I was finished she looked at me a few moments. Then, with a sigh, she picked up her knife and began shelling peas again.

"And you—believe all this?" she asked, not looking at me.

"Don't you?" I asked.

I saw her throat move.

"Don't ask me," she said. "I don't want to think about it. And, if you have any—notions about what's going to happen to me, don't tell me that either."

"I won't."

She looked up. "You mean you *have?*" she asked in a thin voice.

I shook my head. "No."

She went back to her work. "For how long?" she asked. "When will you start on *me?*"

"Honey—"

She put down the knife. "Tom, what are you going to *do?*" she asked. "Is it just going to go on and on like this?"

I couldn't look at her. I had no answer.

"I told you I wouldn't let it hurt you," I said.

"Very funny," she murmured.

I got up and put my cup in the sink. "I'll do something soon," I said. "I don't know what but . . . I will. I promise."

She shrugged and I knew she didn't believe me.

"Will you take back Elsie's paper?" she asked.

"All right."

I left the kitchen and went into the living room. I picked the paper up off the sofa and folded it. I was halfway across the porch when Anne called. I went to the window and asked what she wanted.

"Would you get back the piepans Elsie borrowed?" she asked.

Before it hit me I'd said yes. Then I stood there rigidly, staring through the screen into the living room. I couldn't seem to catch my breath. They were such simple words. Get back the piepans Elsie borrowed. They were absurdly simple. Yet they made me feel as if I were being lowered into a pit of lunacy in which not only the mundane objects around me were sources of horror but even the most ordinary of words spoken between people.

At first I was going to go back into the house, say I felt sick again and would she get the piepans herself? But I knew that would sound false and start her all over again on a treadmill of suspicions and fears. So I found myself turning, walking around the house and starting up the alley beside Elsie's house, although my flesh cringed from it.

It was the dream all over again. Late afternoon, the sky a hazy light, and me walking up on the porch and knocking; almost expecting to find that sign on the door. Elsie opening the door.

The yellow housecoat clinging to her body; it wasn't wet. That was the only difference.

"Hi," she said.

"I brought your paper," I said mechanically. It sounded like someone else's voice.

"Oh. Good." She took it.

I stood there.

"Something else?"

"You have—" I swallowed hard. "You have our piepans?" I asked.

"Oh, yes." She turned.

I looked automatically toward the lower cupboard— and felt my scalp prickle as she stooped down and pulled open the door.

When the housecoat slipped off her right leg, I felt

myself drawing back. Elsie clucked. She tried to cover her leg but the housecoat slid off again. "Oh, well," she said.

With a shudder, I pulled open the door and walked out of the house.

"Where are you going?" I heard Elsie call after me.

I jumped down the porch steps and ran to the foot of the alley, dashed around the end of the fence, past our garage door and around the corner of our house. Only then did I stop and lean weakly against the wall. I was shaking badly. Reality and dream seemed to be running together. I didn't know one from the other. If Helen Driscoll had come walking out of our living room it would have frightened but not surprised me. If I'd seen Elizabeth lying on her lawn with doctors bending over her I might have thought it frightening— but not unbelievable. My breath grew heavier and heavier. I felt my mind approaching some kind of peak.

Suddenly, for some reason, I remembered the pie-pans. They worried me. I couldn't go back without them. Anne would ask me why I hadn't gotten them and I couldn't tell her. I had to get some piepans, I thought wildly. *Any* piepans.

I pushed away from the wall and started running across the lawn. I glanced back automatically and saw Elsie on her back porch, looking at me strangely. She started to say something but I ran faster and went across the street. I jumped the curb and ran across Frank and Elizabeth's lawn. I jumped up onto the porch.

And staggered to a halt.

In on the living-room floor I saw Frank crumpled in a limb-twisted heap, blood gushing in crimson spurts across his white shirt front.

"Frank!"

I burst in through the door, screaming his name a second time.

A flurry of actions then. Me standing in the doorway, gaping down at the empty floor. Elizabeth rushing out of the kitchen, face tight with alarm. Frank running out of the bedroom, saying, "What the—?"

I stood there, weaving dizzily.

"Oh, no," I muttered. "Oh, no."

*You're going mad!* The words clawed at my mind.

"What in the hell's going on?" Frank asked. They both stared at me in amazement. I felt the room rocking and tilting.

"No!" I remember crying out.

Then blackness.

# FIFTEEN

ALAN PORTER FOLDED HIS GOLIATH frame into an oversize leather chair, crossed his legs, put his glasses on the desk and smiled at me.

"Okay," he said, "let's have it. Take your time."

It was Monday night. I'd regained consciousness on Frank and Elizabeth's living room couch, Anne bending over me concernedly. My first reaction had been to stare, then to smile sheepishly. Before we left we told Frank and Elizabeth I hadn't been feeling well all day. It wasn't much of an explanation but they were polite enough to accept it. At least Elizabeth was; Frank didn't look very convinced.

We went home and, after a short, pointed discussion, I'd phoned Alan. He'd told us to come to his office that night. We were there now, Anne waiting tensely in the outer office, me with Alan. Elizabeth was baby-sitting for us.

"Well, you've had a time of it," Alan said after I'd finished my story.

"You remain, as always," I said, "a master of the understatement."

He smiled. "Quite so." Then he shook his head and clucked.

"The fantastic potential of the human mind," he said.

I didn't reply. I didn't think I was supposed to.

Alan straightened up in his chair.

"Well, to start," he said, "you're not, of course, losing your mind."

I hadn't thought I was either but a tremor of relief went through me to hear verification from such authoritative lips.

"Which begs the question," I said.

"What is it," he asked, "exactly?" He knit his fingers together and flexed them a moment.

"As far as the hypnosis goes," he said, "it couldn't of course, have bestowed any unique power on you. What it might have done is, shall we say, released an already latent power.

"Which is not to say," he went on, raising a hand as I began to speak, "that this is anything unnatural. It's doubtless a case of what psi investigators choose to call the *supernormal*—as distinguished from the old hackneyed term, *supernatural*. It's a lot easier to deal with proceedings which fit into the natural scheme of things than it is to deal with beyond-the-pale marvels. Miracles are out of fashion."

"No ghosts then," I said, "no powers of divination."

He smiled.

"I think not," he said. "No matter how apparently weird the occurrence, there's a relatively natural explanation for it. I say relatively because there are, of course, basic predications to be accepted—such as the existence of telepathy and its supplements—clairvoyance, psychometry, et cetera. The so-called *para*—or beyond—*normal* abilities of the human mind."

"But . . . me?" I said. "Why should I have them?" I hadn't told him about my father. Somehow that minor parlor trick seemed inconsequential now.

"You or anyone," Alan said, slowly. "This goes beyond particular heredity." He looked amused. "Which makes me, I might add, something of a rebel in my profession; luckily for you. There are those of my colleagues through whose minds, I fear, the term schizophrenia might well be running now in regard to you."

"I wouldn't blame them," I said. "Now that I look back, I've behaved rather weirdly this past week."

"I'd say so," Alan said.

He shifted in his chair.

"Well, now," he said, "before tackling details it might be well for me to pass along a few generalizations I think would be of interest to you."

"Shoot."

"You see," he began, "mental evolution has followed a definite pattern. Formlessness first. Struggling consciousness. Instinct. Little individuality of function; much collectivity. The primitive mental state.

"Next came a deletion of broadening response. Maximum limitation in exchange for maximum direction and power. In a word—focus. The state we're pretty much existing in at the moment. We're absolute masters of technique and, conversely, absolute fumblers at self-knowledge.

"The final step, the step yet to come or, perhaps, already in the making, is this: To retain the values of rationality, of objectivity; yet—at the same time—to re-plunge back into the formless irrational again. What will appear to be a step backward will actually be a step forward into subjective speculation. The step toward self-direction. Toward, in short, awareness."

He smiled.

"Such a mouthful," he said. "You get the drift, though."

"Sort of," I said. "Are you—leading up to saying that . . . what happened to me was a sort of mechanical speed-up of this evolutionary trend?"

"Not exactly," he said, "although I think the hypnosis—or, more accurately, the faulty extraction of your mind from hypnosis—did tap your latent powers of dissociation. Or, putting it in another way, unlocked your psychical double-jointedness. Your psi."

I must have looked confused for he said, "I've used that word twice now. Probably it throws you. What it's accepted as meaning is simply this: the mental function by which paranormal cognition takes place."

"I say 'oh,' " I said.

He grinned briefly.

"Which brings us to a particular," he said. "A tangential point accepted by only a few; among them, me."

He shifted in his chair and looked fixedly at me.

"You recall," he said, "that, a moment ago, when you asked why you? I said, you or anyone. This is a prime point. I believe that every single human being is, from birth, endowed with varying degrees of psychic perceptivity—and needs only a touch to its mechanism to use this perceptivity in responding to experience.

"Naturally," he went on, "this power is little suspected. The entire concept, for that matter, is pretty disreputable at the moment. And, because it is, not very much in evidence. Like many a human response, it needs loving attention to bring it out. The negative approach hurts it. It's not a measurable factor which can be examined whether one believes in it or not—

that's the tricky part of it. The part which makes it, scientifically, suspect. I do believe, however, that in time men will realize the existence of their psi, and in so realizing be able to reactivate their too-long un-realized potentialities."

"You know," I said, "that's odd. Because there've been times when I could have sworn that Richard knew what I was thinking—and knew that I knew what *he* was thinking."

"More than possible," Alan said. "Until children acquire the power of verbal communication, they very likely make a more or less undirected use of their nat-ural telepathic powers.

"Which," he went on, "also applies historically. I believe that, in primitive times, before verbal com-munication became established, these paranormal tal-ents were commonplace. It stands to reason. Could all the human needs be conveyed by grunts and shoves?"

"Then, when people began speaking to each other," I said, "these abilities were lost?"

"Not so much lost, I think," he said, "as repressed. I believe they still exist in us, faint echoes of their former vitality."

He paused and looked at me in silence for a mo-ment.

"As to your particular case," he said, "I think that the perceptivity released in you is more akin to that of the primitives than it is to that of the, shall we say, man of tomorrow. But don't feel too badly about that. Ninety-five per cent of the so-called mediums are in the same boat—though they'd be double-damned be-fore they'd admit it. Their actions prove it, however; the disorderly, directionless, pointless ramblings of their séances; the absurd contradictory results they so often get.

"Which is why," he continued, "these things which

have been happening to you have come unexpectedly, without warning except for that occasional physical heightening—which heightening is *also* proof of its imperfection. The fully developed mediums don't have this depleting physical aftereffect you've been having. Their perceptivity is strictly mental. It comes, if we choose to put it this way, from the brain, not the guts. And in addition, of course, it is at all times under strict control. It doesn't creep up on them. They call all the shots."

"Well, I guess it's a sort of comfort," I said, "to know that there are others who've gone through the same things I have."

"Plenty of them," Alan said, "and, although they would likely call it a 'psychic gift,' I'd call it more an affliction. In its lack of self-direction and self-understanding, in its inchoate, disjointed functioning, it does far more harm than good."

"Amen to that," I said.

He smiled at the grim sound in my voice, then went on.

"Think of it this way," he said. "You—and the great majority of undeveloped mediums—are traversing a dark tunnel with a flashlight that goes on occasionally—completely beyond your control. You catch fleeting glimpses of what's around you, never knowing what you're going to see, never knowing when you're going to see it."

"Doesn't sound very promising," I said.

"It's a beginning," he said. "But, as to details: they all come down to one thing, I believe—telepathy or aspects of same. You knew when that can of tomatoes hit your wife on the head, because she transmitted the thought of pain to you—and you converted it back into physical sensation.

"You were tuned into the baby-sitter's mind and, in a sense, knew what she was going to do and acted on it. Similarly with your lady neighbor. You tapped her mind several times—then dreamed up a conclusion to her 'overhead' desires."

"But the housecoat," I said, "the piepans."

"All known to you," he said. "Was that the first time she'd ever worn that housecoat?"

"No. I'd seen it before but—"

"Well then, the chances of her wearing it were pretty high. And, as for the piepans, well, they'd been borrowed; sooner or later they had to be gotten back. You also knew that."

"But Anne sending me for them," I said.

"Who made you stay home today," he asked, "Anne or you? You set it up yourself."

"She might have gone herself."

"Maybe she'd decided to ask you before you even dreamed what you did. So you knew she wanted you to go for them. Then, too, there's also the possibility that your mind is making what happens match the dream."

"Like that train wreck?" I challenged.

"Clairvoyance," he said, "another aspect of telepathy. You more than likely telepathized with someone present at the actual wreck. This very often happens when such a catastrophe occurs. And that telepathizing took the form of a quite vivid dream."

"What about the comb then," I asked, "the poker?"

"As for the comb this is another adjunct of telepathy. It's called *psychometry*. An ability whereby the medium holds an object belonging to the person he telepathizes with and 'learns' things about that person. The object, somehow, acts as an aid to thought-transference. In this case it was a comb. The death idea you got was clearly Elizabeth's—I think you said that was her name. Pregnant women often have this

conscious or subconscious fear all through gestation—
for themselves, for their unborn child.

"And, as for the poker, well the same thing—except
that we don't know whose mind you were beginning
to pick. Or what connection the poker had with them.
If you wanted to find out you'd have to pick it up
again."

"Not me," I said, shaking my head, remembering
the jolt of nausea it had brought.

"Can't say I blame you," he said, "although that
would be the only way."

"What about knowing Anne's mother had—died?"

"Telepathy," he said, "or maybe, in this case, pure
coincidence. Your wife had, after all, just told you that
her mother was ill. You knew her mother was old and
had been ill several times in the past year. No mystery
for you to believe she might be dead. The phone call
only added to the intrigue."

"But—"

"Or, as I said," he continued, "it might have been
telepathy. From Anne's father—or from her dying
mother. Both are possible."

"And . . . seeing my neighbor on the floor of his
living room?"

"You told me that, at that party, there was a comment made about Elizabeth shooting her husband.
That was in your mind. You also know about her
husband's secret affair. A simple thing for a stimulated
mind to put these two together and come up with a
vision of your neighbor shot."

"What if it happens, though?" I asked.

"It will prove nothing except that Elizabeth has
shot her husband. It will be no more prophecy on
your part than if you predicted the death of three
hundred people on July fourth and they obliged by
killing themselves in traffic accidents. Here you're
dealing with percentages, which is a very different

matter. And, offhand, I'd say that the percentages of Elizabeth shooting her husband are rather high—especially if they have a gun in the house. Do they?"

I stared at him a moment.

"Frank has a Luger," I said. "He got it in Germany."

"Let's hope it's been inactivated," Alan said.

"Well . . ." I shook my head. "Which of their minds was I reading then in seeing what I did?"

"Elizabeth's perhaps," he said, "or, since you don't think that she knows about her husband's affair, her husband's mind. The fear of guilt. He thinks about his wife shooting him for revenge. You pick it up and your aggravated mind composes a scene in which that very thing has occurred. You 'see' this scene."

I leaned back in the chair.

"It all sounds so damned simple," I said.

"Not at all," Alan said. "You've been the intimate witness to some wonderful things, Tom—itemized proofs of telepathy and its several manifestations. This is no little thing."

I sat silently a few moments, trying to come up with something. It seemed impossible that all that terror, all that incredible experience could be so easily explained, so quickly written off. Maybe I was a little disappointed. On the surface I agreed with him; it was more harm than good. Underneath there was still that childish, half longing for it to be something unusual. Something magic.

"And the woman?" I said.

"Telepathy," he said, "which, doubtless, came from this woman—what's her name?"

"Helen Driscoll."

"Exactly. You're probably right in your assumption that she wishes she were in that house again and you're picking up the desire. Then, too, it is just possible she left in the house a sort of energized memory which you've tapped. But that's only a shot in the dark. The other answer is much more feasible."

"No ghosts then," I said, smiling wryly.

"No ghosts," he said.

I sighed. I confessed to him that I had, for a short time, believed that I'd come across proof of life after death. Alan smiled.

"It would be comforting," he said, "if such proof existed. Unfortunately, it doesn't—no matter what our avid spiritualist friends claim. Telepathy is still the answer as far as I'm concerned. For *all* paranormal phenomena."

He leaned back in his chair and put his hands behind his head.

"Yes," he said, "it would be very nice to believe in a simple, contiguous pattern. A continuous life force existing in an endless cyclic phase between latency and activity, action and withdrawal, incarnation and nonincarnation, life and—as we put it—death. Nice to think that the word is a misnomer."

He shrugged.

"We can't do that, I'm afraid," he said. "Not, that is, with assurance, not with scientific honesty. It may seem a beautifully unencumbered theory, simple and right. But that doesn't make it provable." He smiled. "It isn't provable," he said.

He took down his hands and picked up his glasses again.

"Now," he said, "let's hypnotize you again and get those bugs out of your head."

I repeat: Famous last words.

# SIXTEEN

ANNE MET ME AT THE DOOR WHEN I got home from work the next afternoon. She kissed me and looked inquiringly at me. I smiled.

"I guess it worked," I said.

There was a moment's suspension. Then she pressed close and hugged me. "Thank God," she murmured.

We went into the kitchen and, while she continued making supper, I told her that, as far as I could see, Alan had removed whatever it was that had been plaguing me. I'd not only not dreamed the night before, I'd slept peacefully and waked greatly refreshed. In addition, the day had been spent at work without one intrusion on my mind. In that respect, at least, I was an island unto myself again.

"It's still hard to believe," Anne said, "that just one visit to Alan could stop it."

"It only took one visit with your brother to start it," I said.

"I guess," she said. "Well, I think Alan is marvelous."

"He'd deny that," I said. "You know what he said."

I'd told her how Alan had, quickly and efficiently, put me under hypnosis and "smoothed out a few psychic wrinkles with the palm of suggestion." I'd been conscious of a decided change as soon as I came out of the trance. The tension was gone; there was only a sense of abundant well-being. Which still remained with me and, quite obviously, was removing a weight from Anne's mind.

"He'll never know how relieved I am," she said. "I really don't know how long I could have taken it. I'm—still not over mother's . . . death. And—"

I got up and went over to her. I put my arms around her and she leaned against me tiredly.

"It's been a terrible week for you," I said. "I'll try to make it up to you."

She smiled and patted my cheek.

"You're back," she said. "That's the most important thing."

"I'm back," I said.

While I changed clothes I told her how Alan was going to write up the case in one of the psychiatric journals ("using only your initials, of course"). The entire matter had been intriguing to him.

I was going into the bathroom when Anne called.

"If you're going in there to wash up," she said, "don't. The sink's clogged up. It just finished emptying about half an hour ago. It took all day."

"Did you tell Sentas?" I called back.

"I've been phoning him all day," she said, "but they've been out. You want to try again?"

"All right." I went back into the hall and dialed Sentas' number.

His wife answered. "Hello?"

"Mrs. Sentas, this is Tom Wallace next door," I said. "Is your husband there?"

"One moment, please," she said. She set down the receiver and I heard the muffled sound of her receding footsteps. Faintly, I heard her call, "Harry!"

In a few moments, Sentas picked up the receiver.

"What is it?" he asked.

"The, uh, bathroom sink is clogged up, Mr. Sentas," I said. "It takes hours and hours to empty."

"Your kid drop something in it?" he asked.

"I don't think so," I answered, "and . . . we'd appreciate it if you'd take a look at it—or have it fixed; either one."

"I just got home," he said. "I haven't even had supper yet."

"Well . . . after supper then?" I asked. "We're really in a fix without the use of it."

In the short period of silence that followed I could almost see the hard and irritated expression on his face.

"I'll stop by later," he said.

"Thank you," I said. But he'd already hung up.

I went into the kitchen.

"As cordial as ever," I said. "He's really a charmer."

Anne smiled a little.

"Maybe he's got troubles too," she said.

"Maybe." I went to the window and looked out. I saw Richard and Candy in the next yard. They were sitting in Candy's sand box, digging with spoons.

"They play together very well, don't they?" I said.

"Huh," was my wife's quiet comment.

"What is the meaning of *huh*?"

"The meaning is they fight so much all day that,

by the time you get home from work, they're too weak to fight."

"Richard fights?"

"Well, I'll use my parent's prerogative and say that it's usually Candy's fault. As a matter of fact, it usually is. She gets no disciplining at all."

"That's too bad," I said, watching them play.

"Tom, when do you want to go to the store," Anne asked, changing the subject, "tonight?"

"Got much to get?" I asked.

"Quite a bit," she said. "We missed last week. When I got hit on the head."

"Oh, that's right. Well . . . how much time is there before supper?"

"I'm making beef pie. So it'll be another hour at least."

"Okay. I'll go now, then. Incidentally, how is your head?"

"Fine."

"Funny if *you* started reading minds now," I said.

"Hilarious," she said.

I patted her back as I walked past her. I got the grocery pad and pencil from the drawer and took it back to the table. I sat down and opened it.

"What'd you do with my scribblings?" I asked.

"I have them in a box," she said.

"We'll show them to our grandchildren," I said.

Anne tried to smile. I realized that she was still mourning for her mother so I said no more. I picked up the pencil and drew six thin rectangles to represent the counters of the market. I'd write the items Anne named off on the counter which displayed it. It was a habit I'd picked up the first year of our marriage. It saved retraced steps and, in the vastnesses of the L.A. supermarkets, that can add up to miles and minutes.

"What first?" I asked.

"Let's see," she said. "Well, we need sugar, flour, salt, pepper."

"Hold it." I wrote them down in their appropriate places. "Go on," I said then.

"Butter. Bread."

I wrote them down. "And?" I said.

"Orange juice. Eggs. Bacon."

"Got it."

"A variety of soups," she said, "a variety of cereals."

I wrote them down. I looked up at her. "Yes," I said, "what el—?"

I stopped dead and looked at my hand. It was writing.

*By itself.*

I felt sure my hair was rising. I sat there gaping at the moving pencil, at what it was writing. Only vaguely did I hear what Anne was saying.

The pencil stopped.

"Huh?" I started sharply and looked over at Anne.

"I said did you get that last?"

"No. No. I was—still on the other." She hadn't seen then.

"You asked me what else," she said.

"I know. I just—forgot one."

"I said soda crackers, butter, cookies and peanut butter," she said.

"All right." I managed to keep my voice calm.

While Anne was looking into the cupboard to see what else we needed, I quickly crossed out the words I'd written across the page—realizing, as I did, that it wasn't my handwriting. Then I went on transcribing the groceries she named. I didn't tell her; I knew I mustn't. It's an accident, I kept telling myself. It's just a faint carry-over. It doesn't mean a thing.

Ten minutes later I was in the car heading for the market; staring straight ahead and thinking about those words I'd written; unable to efface them from my mind.

*I am Helen Driscoll.*

Sentas didn't come till past nine.

Before then I stayed out in the garage working on Richard's wagon which needed new bolts and repainting. I didn't feel like doing it; I'd put it off for weeks. But I couldn't stay in the house. I was afraid something else might happen.

I say "afraid" yet it was different somehow. It was not for myself that I feared now. It was Anne. It didn't take telepathy or anything approaching it for me to be fully aware of the state of her nerves. She'd had more than her share of shocks that past week. Even under normal conditions the death of her mother—to whom she was very close—coupled with the pressure of living with a man who'd gone through what I had was enough to break the sturdiest spirit. That all this should have taken place during a period of pregnancy marked by extreme nervous tension had made it five times as bad. I simply couldn't tell her what I'd written down. I was afraid to.

While I painted the wagon I kept thinking about those words.

I couldn't imagine what they signified. That I had seen Helen Driscoll was one thing and, in the way Alan had put it, very explicable. But to receive what appeared to be a message from her—and in, apparently, her own handwriting—this went far beyond credulity.

Yet, I was not so much alarmed for myself as for Anne. For some reason (my visit to Alan, of course) I sensed a difference in myself. That wary, glancing-over-the-shoulder condition was gone. Being concerned for Anne, however, was quite enough. I hoped, for her sake, there would be no more incidents.

There were, of course. And not long in coming either. At least she wasn't there when the first one occurred. I'll always be grateful for that.

It was about ten minutes before nine when she came out into the garage and told me that Richard was asleep and would I keep an eye on him while she went over to help Elizabeth get a bobbin threaded in her sewing machine? I said I would and, after she'd gone, I went back in the house. It was just dark.

I sat in the kitchen, the grocery pad in front of me.

I kept picking up the pencil and rolling it tentatively between my fingers. As had been the case from the start of all this, curiosity was still an important factor. I think you may understand that. No matter what had happened, the interest was still there. It was unavoidable.

I had just decided to try the writing again when I heard a thump on the front door. I started and put down the pencil quickly. Then, thinking it might conceivably be Anne carrying something and unable to open the door, I put the pencil into its little holder on the side of the pad and dropped them both back into the drawer.

It was Sentas, looking jaded and put upon.

"Hello," I said.

"Still clogged?" he asked brusquely.

"Still." I stepped aside so he could come in. He entered as if I were an intruder in his house; not its tenant.

He went right into the bathroom and started running the water. The sink began to fill up; it didn't drain at all. Sentas kept running the water, staring fixedly at its mounting surface. Don't you think it might be a good idea to turn it off now? I thought. He didn't. He kept it running until the bowl was almost full. Only then did he twist off the faucet.

"Hmmm," he said. He looked at the water. He

reached under its surface and tapped a big finger on the drain hole. He looked disgusted.

"Your wife wash her hair lately?" he asked.

"I don't know," I said.

"Hair clogs it up," he said.

"I see. Well . . . what are we going to do?"

He blew out a weary gust of breath. "I can't do anything now," he said.

You managed to fill the damn sink, I thought irritably.

"I'll . . . call a plumber in the morning," he said reluctantly.

"Is it too late to get one now?" I asked.

"Yeah." He started into the hall. "I'll call one in the morning."

Which was when it happened; all the more horrible because it came without warning, because it followed so closely on the heels of our mundane discussion regarding the clogged sink.

"Sentas," we heard.

Sentas froze. So did I.

"Sentas. Harry Sentas," said the voice.

I felt myself shuddering.

"You know me, Harry Sentas."

*It was the voice of my two-year-old son.*

Yet not his voice. It came from his vocal cords, yes, but it was another's voice. Have you ever seen a marionette show where the adult operators speak in piping voices, supposedly through the immobile lips of their stringed dolls? It was like that; like the voice of a dummy speaking in the distorted falsetto of its ventriloquist master.

"You know me, Harry Sentas. You know me."

Sentas drew in a ragged breath. His face was blank, losing color.

"What the hell is this?" he asked in a trembling, guttural voice.

I opened my mouth to answer but nothing came out.

"You know me, Harry Sentas," said my son, said the voice. "My name is Helen Driscoll."

Sentas and I both jolted with shock at the same time. He started for the bedroom, then stepped back as if executing some grotesque dance step. He whirled on me.

"What is this, a gag?" he challenged.

"I swear to—" I muttered.

"You know me, Harry Sentas," said the voice.

Sentas glared at me for a long moment. Then, abruptly, he turned and walked across the living room floor.

"Damn jokes," he snapped. "Fix your own sink!"

The house shook with the crash of the slamming front door.

I moved into the bedroom on numbed legs; to the side of Richard's crib. I heard him muttering in the darkness.

"Come back," he said in that hideous, doll voice. "Come back, Harry Sentas."

Then he was still. A great shuddering breath passed through him and he slept again, heavily and undisturbed.

I was sitting on the sofa when Anne got back.

I think she knew from the instant she saw me.

"No," she said feebly, "oh, no." There was a sadness in her voice; a tired, capitulating sadness.

"Anne, sit down," I said.

"No."

"Honey, please. Don't run away from it. That will only make it worse."

She stood there trembling, staring at me.

"Sit down," I said. "Please."

"No."

*"Sit down."*

She came over and sat on the other end of the sofa, perched on the edge of the cushion like a fearful but obedient child. She gripped at her forearms with whitening fingers.

"I'm telling you this," I said, "because—well, if it happens to you and you haven't been told, it may frighten you."

She covered her eyes suddenly and began to cry.

"Oh . . . God help us," she sobbed. "I thought it was over, I thought it was over."

"Honey, don't."

She looked up, teeth clenched, a look almost deranged on her face.

"I can't take much more," she warned in a voice that was all the more frightening for its softness. *"I can't take much more."*

"Anne, maybe—"

I stopped nervously. For one hideously forgetful instant I'd been about to suggest she go to her mother's until this thing was settled.

"Maybe what?" she asked.

"Nothing. I—"

"Oh, are we going to have the s-secrets again?" she asked and I could tell from the sound of her voice how close to the edge she was. "The little secrets?"

"Honey, listen," I begged. "If we face this thing now we can—"

"Face it!" she exploded. "What have I been doing! I've been living with it! Dying with it! I can't stand any more!"

I shifted quickly to her side and held her shaking body against me.

"Shhh, baby," I whispered futilely, "don't. It'll be all right. It's different now, it's different. I'm not helpless anymore." The words seemed to flow out of me and, even as they did, I knew that they were true. "I can control it now, Anne. It can't hurt us if we only face it. Believe me, I'm not helpless anymore."

"Well, I am," she sobbed. "I *am*."

I held her for a long time without speaking. And, during that time, I made a decision; a decision I knew had been inevitable. It made sense to me now. What I'd said to Anne was true. I was sure of it. I wasn't a helpless pawn now.

I was going to make things work my way.

# SEVENTEEN

**B**UT I COULDN'T TELL ANNE ANYTHING then. She was too upset. All the built-up tension in her seemed to have burst its shell and there was no stopping it. The death of her mother, the shocks heaped upon her because of me; then, the off-guard relaxing when she thought it was done with and, in this off-balanced state, a second plunging into dread. It would have broken anyone.

I put her to bed with a sedative and stayed with her until she'd fallen into a heavy sleep. As soon as I was sure she was asleep I went back into the kitchen and got the grocery pad. There was something more to this than Alan had said. If Helen Driscoll wanted to be living here again why should I be getting written messages from her? Most importantly, why should she be speaking through the mouth of my child? And to her brother-in-law?

Unless something had happened to her back east. Unless she was—

*No.* I fought that. I wasn't ready to topple off that brink again. It was a trap. I had to face this thing hardheadedly this time; not with a gullible willingness to swallow, in an instant, what philosophers spent lifetimes seeking out. I wasn't going to make the same mistake again. All I would admit was that there was more to the situation than Alan and I had thought.

I picked up the pencil and held it lightly on the paper. I looked out through the door window. That was what you had to do in what is called automatic writing. It is beyond will, beyond conscious penmanship. People have read while they were writing. Some have slept.

I tried to take my attention off the pencil. I wanted to put it out of my mind in order to allow my subconscious to control it. I stared into Elsie's kitchen and saw her sitting there with Ron and her parents. They were playing their weekly game of bridge. I saw Elsie's face contort with a wild laugh and heard, floating through the window, the sound of it. I wondered if their noise would distract me, then realized that distraction was precisely what I wanted. I paid careful attention to Elsie.

I thought about the times I'd seen into her knotted little mind. I thought what a terrible world it would be if men realized their potential overnight, and everyone knew what everyone else was thinking. What a terrible breakdown of society. There could *be* no society when every man was an open book to his neighbors. Unless, of course, by the time such a condition prevailed, men could gain maturity and be able to cope with their new-found abilities.

An hour passed. My hand grew cramped and began to ache; but the pencil remained motionless.

Another hour passed. Abruptly, I gave it up. Obviously, nothing was going to come of it. While I was getting into my pajamas it occurred to me that Helen Driscoll was becoming more tenuous all the time. One moment she was appearing to me; the next speaking with the tongue of my child; the next commandeering my hand and writing that it was she. If she was a spirit—and I wouldn't admit that even to myself— she was a very confused one. The thought made me smile. Was it possible? I thought that, certainly, it was. Presuming survival, the fact that people retained their personal consciousness beyond death would in no way guarantee sudden omniscience to them. If anything, this abrupt immersion in limbo would probably jar them frighteningly. I'd read once, in a book on spiritualism, the souls often refuse to admit they are dead and attempt continued existence on their prior level. Thus, if Helen Driscoll were—

I broke that off urgently. I wasn't going into it. I decided that, for my immediate problem, I had best try the original method of contacting Helen Driscoll— actually to see her. I felt no qualms about this now. I didn't fear any physical depletion. Perhaps—I suspected it—I was becoming, at least in part, what Alan had called a "developed" medium, one who was not helpless prey to his awareness. I had no idea of why this should be so.

It was about twelve-forty when I sat on the sofa, turned out the lights and began to concentrate.

I didn't put back my head or close my eyes. I felt that these gestures were extraneous. Probably it wasn't necessary to turn out the lights either; hadn't Alan said something about true mediums' having quite successful manifestations even in broad daylight? I had also read, however, that light weakens psychic phenomena and decided to take the easiest way. I was, after all, still a novice.

My search for Helen Driscoll was not a positive,

thrusting process. I didn't murmur—Where are you? If you're there, rap the coffee table leg, once for yes, twice for no. In a sense, I merely emptied my mind of nonessentials and waited for her to manifest herself. I was no general marshaling his psychic forces, but only a medium through which they could express themselves.

It was in that semi-dormant state that the intrusions began. Since I was attempting to contact Helen Driscoll I wasn't looking for what happened.

Which was a sense of tension, a double feeling—of dismay and reaction to that dismay. I shifted on the sofa and looked around as if I expected to see her in the room. But there was nothing. Only this feeling of restless malaise, similar to what I'd felt that first night. Yet different now. My system only mirrored the feeling; the tension was elsewhere than myself.

I thought it had to do with Helen Driscoll. I tried to apply it thus. Was it her feeling, her emotion? I couldn't tell; but it didn't seem to fit. There was an aura about it that was alien to her. Still I fumbled with it. Was she upset, was she having trouble in revealing herself to me? Trouble getting through this way now that I was not as I had been?

I started to rise to get the pad and pencil again.

Pure animal emotion hit my mind and I sat back down heavily. It was too strong, too close. It expanded fluidly, running together before my mind, settling into brief cohesion, breaking up. As if what I saw were reflections in water and someone was plunging his hand into it, dispelling the image just before it came together.

Still unaware, I thought only of Helen Driscoll. It was her emotion I felt, I was sure. She was trying to convey something to me; but what I couldn't tell. It was vague and inchoate; it wouldn't hold together. There was anger; violent anger; there was resentment, hatred. But against whom I couldn't tell either. I was only sure it was Helen Driscoll. Maybe, the idea came, she resented Sentas for some reason. After all, she'd spoken to him saying, *You know me, Harry Sentas*.

All sorts of conjectures passed quickly across my conscious mind, obscuring impressions. Conjectures that she had been close to her sister and Sentas had resented that closeness and, by unpleasant behavior, forced her to leave. That she was in love with Sentas and, rather than face the inevitable shame of having it slip out in the presence of her sister, had left. Even that Sentas had been having an affair with her and that Mrs. Sentas had found out about it and that was why Helen Driscoll left this house. And why there was always a seeming air of strain between Sentas and his wife. As if they were actors portraying a well-adjusted couple, erring in their characterization in the direction of over-formality.

I kept thinking this and it kept distorting the images further, breaking them up into unintelligible smears. The only things which remained constant were the waves of mounting fury.

Suddenly, frighteningly, I thought that it was Anne; and that the object of the animosity was me.

I tried to fight that but the concept stuck. It could so very well be, I knew. In her despair, in her possible twisted resentment of having expressed her innermost hopes to me in vain, in the general tension of being pregnant in this house of shocks—she might very well, under the morality-relaxing influence of sleep, be releasing currents of hatred toward me.

I stood. I sat down again. I couldn't believe it. I couldn't.

The fury rose. Words, like bodiless limbs, flopped past, at first too disjointed, too pointless to understand. I tried hard to understand them and over-concentration weakened them further. I realized quickly that I had to relax. I tried. Impressions jumped across my mind again. Words. *Cruel. Heartless. Home. Wife, you. Scorn for. Brutal and I. You just don't know* . . .

And then *adultery*.

Suddenly I knew. And, in knowing, it seemed as if a million fragments of mirror fell together and I could see the true reflection. I gasped.

The hall light clicked on.

I started violently. On the carpet of light that flooded across the living room floor, my wife came walking slowly.

"Tom?" she asked.

A terrible moment. A moment of being suspended in two places at once—of being conscious of two separate but simultaneous events.

"Tom, are you in there?" Pale-voiced, frightened-voiced.

*"Don't."* It was all I could say.

"Tom, what—" She stopped and I saw her form get hazy and indistinct before my eyes. The other scene flared into clarity.

*Frank and Elizabeth* . . .

Then Anne was clear again. I saw her hand reach up in tiny, hitching movements and press against her cheek.

"What are you doing?" she asked in a faint, trembling voice.

I didn't speak. I was watching Elizabeth's anguish-deranged face as she looked at Frank. His half-sullen, half-shocked look in return.

*She knew about him.*

"Tom, what are you doing?" Anne's voice rang out piercingly in the dark room. It pulled me back. Suddenly I heard the rustle of her nightgown in the darkness and one of the end table lamps flared on. She was bent over it, face taut, looking at me.

"What are you doing!"

"It's Elizabeth," I heard myself saying hoarsely. And, as I said it, suddenly I recalled Alan's words: *Let's hope it's been deactivated.*

"Oh, my God!" I whirled and lunged for the door.

"Where are you going!" her voice rose shrilly.

"I've got to—!" I didn't finish. I jerked open the door and started out, barefooted.

"Tom!" The sound of her broken cry was terrible. For an instant I hesitated, drawn to her despairing need.

Then the shot rang out.

# EIGHTEEN

**W**ITH A GASP I LEAPED OFF THE porch onto the cold, wet grass and raced toward the curb.

I was halfway across the street when the second shot exploded in the night. I clamped my teeth together and tried to run faster. I leaped the curb and rushed across their lawn. The light from a single lamp illuminated their living room.

*Alan was wrong.* For some reason that was the first thing I thought as I jolted to a halt and stared in through the window.

Because Frank was lying crumpled on the living room floor—*in exactly the position I'd seen him in that day.* Everything was the same; the twisted pain on his face, the eyes staring, the blood pulsing across the front of his white shirt.

There was one difference.

Elizabeth stood like a statue in the hall doorway,

the Luger held in her hand, on her face a wild and stricken look. In the silence I could hear the clicking sound as she pulled the trigger again and again.

When I ran in, her head snapped around and she stared at me an instant before pitching forward on the rug without a sound. I heard the Luger thump on the rug.

After that it was all movement and confusion.

I ran to Frank and knelt beside him, feeling for a heartbeat. It was there; faintly. Only one of the bullets had struck him, it appeared, but it was a bad chest wound. I pushed up, the blood pulsing at my temples, and stepped quickly over Elizabeth. In the hall closet I found clean sheets and pulled one out. As I stepped across Elizabeth again I flung the sheet open and folded it lengthwise. Then, kneeling by Frank, I wrapped it around him as gently as I could. He groaned softly while I was doing it. He was unconscious now, his eyes closed.

The next thing I did was run into the hall and phone for an ambulance. That done, I managed to get the dead weight of Elizabeth on the couch. Her face was waxen and cool to the touch. I opened the collar of her pajama top and began chafing her wrists. I was doing this when her eyes flickered open.

She stared at me a moment as if she'd never seen me in her life. Then, abruptly, she pushed up.

"Frank!" she gasped.

I held her back. "Lie down, Elizabeth, lie down," I told her.

"No. No."

She fought me, her eyes on Frank, her shoulders pressing violently against my hands. She kept saying Frank's name.

Then, suddenly, the strength seemed to empty from her and she fell back on the couch pillow. Her eyes closed tightly and a long, wavering sigh passed her pale lips. I didn't realize what was happening.

I was checking Frank again when I heard footsteps outside. I thought it was Anne but it turned out to be the man who lived in the house on the right.

"What happ—?" he started to say, then stopped, his mouth open. "Holy Christ," he muttered slowly. He stood there staring at Frank.

In a short while Anne did come, wearing her top-coat. Her only reaction was to look blankly at Frank a moment, then at me. Then she sat down beside Elizabeth and took her hand. I heard Elizabeth's dry, breathless sobbing as I tightened the sheet to stop the bleeding.

The ambulance came five minutes later. The police a few minutes after that.

When we got back to the house, I went into the bathroom to wash my hands. I saw the half-filled sink and, gritting my teeth, I turned to go into the kitchen. I tried to hide my blood stained fingers from Anne as I walked past her. She didn't speak.

I heard the clock strike one as I went in the kitchen. It had been an incredible night. And Alan had said I would probably have nothing to worry about now. There was a grotesque amusement to that.

I was drying my hands when I heard a rustling sound and, looking over my shoulder, I saw Anne standing in the kitchen doorway looking at me. I turned back and hung up the towel. I wondered what she was going to say to me now.. There was not much left in the way of shocks for her.

As I turned from the sink I saw her sit down at the table. I started to walk, then stopped. I leaned back against the sink and we looked at each other.

Finally she spoke.

"Will he die?" she asked, quietly.

It was not what I'd expected to hear. For a moment I could only stare at her.

"I don't know," I said then.

I saw her throat move.

"You know," she said. "You just don't want to tell me."

"No," I said, "I don't know. I thought . . . Elizabeth was going to."

She lowered her eyes. I looked at her a few moments. Then I went over and sat down across from her.

"Look, Anne. I think you know—at least I *hope* you know how badly all of this makes me feel. I'm not a monster, Anne. I'm still the same man you married; believe me. I hate to frighten you. I hate to have all these things happen at a time like this. But I can't help it. Can't you see this? Do you think I'm doing this deliberately? Do you think I'm trying to hurt you? What's happened to me wasn't my doing. I'm just as victimized by it as you are. I don't know what it means or why it should happen to me. But it *is* happening, Anne. I've faced that fact. It's established. And it isn't going to stop. I feel certain of that. I can't imagine what could end it now. It's a part of me. What else can I say? If only you'd accept that; not fight it so hard. It isn't frightening if only you accept it. Believe that, Anne. It isn't terrible then. It can only hurt you if you struggle against it, if you believe it's something unnatural and wrong. Can't you see that?"

I must have sounded pretty impassioned because she looked at me now with sympathy, almost with understanding.

Then it faded.

"What about us?" she asked. "Is it going to be— the same? *Can* it be the same when you're like this? Isn't every day going to be a—a new torture? What if . . . Tom, what if you start seeing things about me, about *us*? I'd know it, Tom, I would. You couldn't hide it, you couldn't pretend you hadn't seen them." She shook her head in short, choppy movements. "How could it work? Life would be unbearable. I'd just be—waiting for something terrible to happen."

"Honey, what happened would have happened anyway. I didn't cause anything. Is that what you've been thinking? How could you? I was aware that they would happen—but I didn't make them happen. Can't you see that?"

She clasped her hands together tightly and looked at them. She bit her lower lip.

"I suppose you're right, but . . ." She looked up at me. "Are you reading my mind now?" she asked.

"Anne, I—" I felt almost speechless. "What in God's name do you think I am, a wizard? No, of course I'm not reading your mind now. I probably couldn't do it if I tried. I told you it was different now. Before it was beyond volition; I picked up things. Now I'd have to concentrate. I don't know what you think it is I can do. But . . . well, believe me, it's not as fantastic as all that. You aren't . . . naked to my mind. Nothing is. I—I . . . I just don't know what to say, Anne."

Breath emptied from her slowly.

"I don't know," she said. "I . . . just don't know either. I don't know if I'm up to it. To live like this every day." She shook her head.

"Honey, it wouldn't be like this every day. Is . . . Elizabeth going to shoot her husband every day? Is your . . . mother . . . ?" I didn't finish.

"What about the woman?" she asked. "Helen Driscoll, if that's who it is."

"That's something that has to be settled," I admitted, "but . . . well, once it is settled . . ."

"And you think you can settle it?"

"I'm going to try, Anne."

She was silent. I could hear the clock ticking hollowly in the cupboard. I sat there a minute. Then I started to get up.

"If I do try," she broke in.

I sat down and looked at her.

"If I try," she said, "will you . . . tell me everything? Everything, Tom?"

"I have told you—"

"I mean everything," she said. "Even about us."

"If you want me to," I said, "of course I will." I reached across the table and took her hand. "I just want you to be with me," I said. "I just don't want you to run away from it any more. I need you, Anne. That hasn't changed."

She tried to smile.

"I've written to my aunt," I said. "I should hear from her soon. Then we'll know if—there's something more to go on. That will make it easier for you, won't it? If you know that it's something in the family?"

She hesitated a moment. Then her hand squeezed mine.

"I'll try, Tom," she said. "I . . . can't say anything more. I think it will frighten me to death but I'll try."

We sat in silence a moment. Then she asked,

"Will he die, Tom?"

"I don't know, Anne," I said. "That's the truth. The sense of death I got had to do with Elizabeth, not Frank. I don't understand that really. But . . . well, it must be him."

She looked at me intently. I saw how she bit her lower lip.

"Tom," she said.

"What?"

"Wh . . . what about me?"

"Honey, I don't know anything about you—or us."

Then I remembered. I smiled at her.

"Unless . . ."

She looked frightened. "What is it?" she asked.

"Would it make you feel too badly," I said, "if I told you I think we're going to have a girl?"

She looked at me, speechless. Then there was a softening around her eyes, a stirring at the corners of her mouth.

"Really?" she murmured.

I held her hands in mine. "I think so," I said. "Does that spoil it? To know, I mean?"

I don't think she heard me. She was looking into the future.

"A girl," she said. "A little baby girl."

The next afternoon when I came home from work Elsie was on her lawn, watering the grass. As I pulled into the driveway she came over.

"Isn't it *awful?*" she said.

I must have looked blank a moment.

"Oh," I said then, "yes. Yes, it is awful."

"We're all so *shocked*," she said. "Such a terrible thing. *Oooh.*" I recognized her shudder. It was the same one she'd affected the night Phil had told her about sticking hatpins into the throats of hypnotized subjects.

"Why should she *do* such a thing?" Elsie asked, "I thought they were so happy."

I didn't need telepathy or any kindred perception to sense plain old female curiosity.

"I really don't know Elsie," I said.

Elsie clucked. "It's so shocking," she said.

"Yes." I turned away.

"Especially about the baby," she said.

For a split second I broke stride and almost stopped. The pleasure I'd felt at not being exposed to her mind was washed away in an instant.

"The—" I started to say, then walked quickly around the corner of the house and went inside.

Anne was in the kitchen scrubbing potatoes.

"The baby?" I asked after I'd kissed her.

She nodded sadly.

"This morning," she said. "I guess it was the shock. She miscarried."

"Oh . . ." I felt sick. The vision had been true after all; the death *had* concerned Elizabeth. More terribly than even I had imagined.

"That poor kid," I said.

"Yes, now she's lost everything."

We were silent a moment.

"Then Frank didn't die," I said.

Anne shook her head.

"No, he'll live." Her lips pressed together bitterly. "He'll live."

We picked up Elizabeth at the hospital two days later. There was no relative to take her home and Frank was still in the hospital. There were no criminal charges against her. Frank had told the police it had been an accident; that they hadn't known the gun was loaded. I guess he felt he had to make amends somewhere—ineffectual as they were.

She was completely uncommunicative when we got to her ward and when we walked her to the car. Anne and I were on each side of her. She walked in slow, faltering steps; as if, overnight, she had become old and infirm.

The ride home was mostly silent. Anne's attempted conversation regarding weather and other innocuous subjects was received either in silence or answered in words so soft they couldn't be heard.

It was during that drive home that I got some of the most awful mental impressions of the entire affair. The most hideous of moments, I discovered then, could take place in bright sunlight, in the most mundane of locations. Night is not a requirement; nor are thunderstorms, high winds or the rain lashed battlements of mad doctors. There were no monsters here; just three human beings. No strange creatures of darkness. No eerie sound or sight. Yet I will never forget the wrenching sickness it gave me.

The feeling came from Elizabeth; of that there was not the least doubt. It began slowly; as a strengthless remorse, a despair, a pitiful longing. It did not remain so very long. Gradually it grew, shooting out tendrils of naked emotion, growing into a horrible weedlike mass of cruel hunger. Higher and higher it mounted. I didn't have to concentrate on it. Emotions that strong overpower you. The emotion of clutching demand, of cold, animal desire, frightening in its intensity.

When the image burst across my mind, I felt myself twitch on the car seat and my hands clamped on the wheel until the blood was forced from them.

The vision was of Elizabeth. She was reaching down with talonlike, trembling hands. She was clawing at Anne's loins. She was ripping open Anne's flesh and tearing loose the child in bloody shreds. She was screaming and screaming. She was tearing her own stitched flesh open—and placing our child inside her body.

I was glad when we got home.

Anne wanted to stay with her but Elizabeth said she'd rather be alone. I felt glad about that. As we walked across the porch we heard her lock the door.

"Tom, will she—do anything to herself?" Anne asked. There was a childlike trust in her voice now; a trust in my ability as a man who could see everything.

I started to answer that she might, then stopped. I knew I had no right to say it. I had no idea what Elizabeth might do.

"I don't know, Anne," I said. "I can't tell. I told you, I'm not a wizard."

"I'm sorry." She took my arm. "I should stay with her, though."

"She'll be all right," I said.

When we got to the house, Anne went next door to Elsie's to see if Richard was still playing all right with Candy. I went up on the porch.

The letter was in the mailbox.

I took it into the living room and read it. I think I smiled a little. It was really an anticlimax now.

When Anne came back, I handed it to her. I saw her lips part as she read it.

"Your grandfather," she said quietly.

"Great-grandfather," I said. "Castor James Wallace of Yorkshire, England. Funny; I'd forgotten all about him. I think my mother told me about him when I was a little boy."

"So he was a medium," Anne said.

"Apparently."

After a few moments, Anne folded the letter and put it into her pocket.

"Well?" I said.

She blew out a soft breath. "Well," she said, "I guess that's it then."

"Do you accept it?" I asked. "Can you live with it now?"

Anne sighed. She looked helpless.

"You're my husband, Madame Wallace," she said.

I hugged her until she groaned. "Easy on Sam," she said. "He doesn't like the pressure."

"Sandra," I said.

I rubbed my cheek against her soft hair. I remembered she'd asked me to tell her everything. Well, I wasn't going to tell her what had been going through Elizabeth's mind. I knew that I might have to temper my promise in the future. There were lies and there were lies.

"Well," she said, after a few moments, "what now?"

"One more thing," I said. "It has to be settled."

"Helen Driscoll?" she asked.

I nodded.

"Helen Driscoll," I said.

# NINETEEN

MRS. SENTAS, ANSWERED THE DOOR. IT was a few minutes past seven that evening.

"Yes?" she said. She spoke in a withdrawn, regal manner.

"May I speak to you and your husband, Mrs. Sentas?" I asked.

"Speak to us about what?" she asked, frowning curiously.

I cleared my throat. "It's—rather delicate," I said. "May I come in?"

She stared at me a while as if she couldn't make up her mind whether I was human or not. Then, with an expression of distaste, she asked, "Is it absolutely necessary? My husband and I are getting ready to go out."

"It's about your sister," I said.

If I had jabbed her with a needle I couldn't have gotten a more forceful twitch from her.

"My—?" She stopped.

"May I come in?" I asked.

Swallowing, she stepped back. I walked past her into the living room and she closed the door.

"Sit down, please," she told me.

I glanced around as I sat on the sofa. It was a duplicate of our living room as far as size went. There the resemblance ended. Where ours was furnished in early-American time-payment, the Sentas' was strictly French provincial and that of the most elegant variety—black-marble-topped tables, antique chairs and sofas, gilded mirrors, thick drapes and thicker carpeting. Without the aid of mediumship I would have laid odds that it was all the result of Mrs. Sentas' taste.

She settled on the edge of a period chair as Mr. Sentas came out of the kitchen, a drink in his hand.

"What's up?" he asked, looking over at me as if I were an intruding salesman.

"Mr. Wallace says he has something to tell us about Helen," said his wife.

"Oh?" Moving to another chair Sentas sat down. *"Well?"* he asked.

I swallowed nervously. It was one thing to make statements to Anne; quite another to sit facing the Sentas' with what I had to say.

"I—wonder," I began, "if you could tell me whether you've heard from your sister lately—"

"Why d'ya ask?" Harry Sentas broke in before I'd finished.

"I have a reason," I said. "Have you?"

"Don't see where it's any of your—" he started.

"Harry." She spoke quietly but it muted him in an instant. I turned to Mrs. Sentas. She looked a trifle drawn.

"Why *do* you ask?" she inquired.

"What'd ya do, open a letter she sent us?" Harry Sentas challenged me.

I looked at her a moment before answering.

"No," I said, glancing at him.

"Mr. Wallace, I asked you a question," Mrs. Sentas said coldly.

I looked at her again. Behind that forbidding exterior I sensed an abject fear.

"I asked, Mrs. Sentas, because I have something to tell you about your sister. But first I have to know if—"

"Tell us what?" she demanded.

"I'm afraid you'll have to bear with me."

"Mr. Wallace I demand to know what you're talking about!"

"I'm talking about your sister, Mrs. Sentas," I said. "I think she's dead."

Mrs. Sentas twitched, then sat motionless.

"What are you talkin' about!" Harry Sentas asked loudly. He put down the glass with a bang and stood up. "Look here, boy!"

"Harry . . ." Her voice faltered as she spoke.

It was silent. I regretted having put it so bluntly even if she had, virtually, forced it from me.

Mrs. Sentas drew in a trembling breath.

"Why do you say she's . . ." She seemed unable to finish.

I braced myself.

"Because," I said, "I've seen her in our house."

"*What?*" Mrs. Sentas leaned forward, her dark eyes stricken.

"I've seen her," I repeated.

Mrs. Sentas shuddered.

"Who the hell d'ya think you are comin' in here with a cock 'n' bull story like that!" Sentas flared. "God damn it, I got half a mind to—!"

"It's not a—" I started.

"I don't know what your game is," he said, pointing at me, "but you better watch it. I'm warnin' ya."

"Harry . . ."

He broke off and looked nervously at Mrs. Sentas. "Look, Mildred," he said, "this is some kind of—" He broke off again—instantly—as she shook her head.

"You haven't heard from her, have you?" I said.

Her voice was hollow. "Not since she went back to New York," she said.

"How long ago was that?"

"Almost a year now."

"Look, fella, we don't want t'hear any more o' this, y'understand?" said Sentas.

"Harry, please."

*"Look,"* he said to his wife, "are we gonna sit here 'n' listen to all this bullsh—" He stopped and glared at me. "You get outa here," he ordered. "Right now!"

I stood up.

"Mr. Wallace, what do you mean, you've seen my sister in your house?" Mrs. Sentas asked, her voice rising.

"I mean what I said," I answered. "I've *seen* her. If you want to see her too be at my house in an hour."

"God damn it, boy, you get the hell outa here!" roared Sentas. He started for me.

"Stay away from me," I said and headed for the door.

"Mr. Wallace!"

I turned. Mrs. Sentas was on her feet, staring at me.

"If this is some kind of joke . . ." she began tensely.

I opened the door. "It's no joke," I said.

Sentas reached the door. He slammed it violently behind me, hitting the heel of my shoe.

"You come back here again, I'll call the cops!" he yelled.

I exhaled wearily as I walked out to the sidewalk. Across the street I saw Elizabeth sitting on her lawn. Anne was standing beside her and both of them were looking across the street at me. Doubtless the noise of the slammed door had attracted them. Anne said something to Elizabeth, then came across the street.

"Well, that was a great big nothing," I said as she came into the house after me.

"They won't come?"

"Hell, no," I said, ruefully. "Sentas practically threw me out of the house. He'll probably evict us next month. That is, *she* will."

Anne clucked. "Now what?" she asked.

I shrugged and blew out a long breath. "Lord knows," I said.

Anne looked at me without saying anything.

"How's Elizabeth?" I asked.

"How could she be?" she asked. "She's alive; no more."

"That poor woman," I said.

"I—told her about . . ."

"What?"

"About what's happened. Not all of it, of course. Just about Helen Driscoll."

"Oh." I shook my head. "That's guaranteed to cheer her up," I said.

"Well, she saw you going into Sentas' house and asked if you were having trouble with them."

I nodded. Then I sank down on the green chair. "Well," I said, "we are exactly nowhere. If only—"

The telephone rang. "Oh, it'll wake up Richard," Anne said hurrying for the hall as fast as she could.

"Hello?" I heard her say quietly. Silence. Then, "Oh?" Pause. "Yes. That's right." Another pause. "Good-bye."

She came back, looking surprised.

"They're coming," she said.

At eight-fifteen the doorbell rang.

"I'll get it," I said. We were in the kitchen finishing up the dishes.

"Tom?"

I stopped in the doorway. "Yes?"

"Will it be—terrible?"

I started to lie, then restrained it. "I don't know, honey," I told her, "honestly, I don't know what will happen. That's why I want you to go over to Elizabeth's house until it's over."

The doorbell rang again. Anne shook her head.

"I won't leave you alone," she said. "If you—go off or something I want to be here."

I smiled. "It could be nothing at all," I said, "but we might as well try to get this thing settled."

The doorbell rang insistently. I could visualize Sentas pushing at it, thin-lipped, impatient.

"You'd better let him in before he kicks it down," Anne said, trying to sound amused.

"No fear of that," I said. "He wouldn't hurt his own property. His wife's property, that is."

I walked across the living room and opened the door.

"Hello," I said.

Sentas grunted. Mrs. Sentas nodded once. They came in and I noted how they stared at the card table and four chairs in the middle of the living room.

Anne came in. "Good evening." she said.

Sentas grunted again. "Mrs. Wallace," said Mildred Sentas, stiffly polite.

"Want to sit down?" Anne invited.

They took their places awkwardly, without comfort.

"Now look," Sentas started before we were seated. "Don't think for a minute we go along with this—story o' yours. We don't. But my wife here's worried about not hearin' from her sister, see? That's why we're here. If this is a joke or anything . . ." He didn't finish. He didn't have to.

"I assure you it isn't a joke," I said.

"Then what is it?" asked Mrs. Sentas. "What did you mean telling us to come over here if we want to see my sister?"

"I meant—"

"And what about your kid talkin' t'me the other night?" accused Sentas. "I suppose that wasn't a joke."

I looked at his angry face.

"You don't really think that was *him* talking, do you?" I asked.

He started to blurt a reply, then sat with his mouth open. "What d'ya mean?" he asked then in a vaguely frightened voice.

"I think it was your sister-in-law," I said.

*"What?"*

"Mr. Wallace, I've had enough of this!" Mrs. Sentas interrupted angrily. "Either you explain yourself or we're leaving!"

"I'll be glad to explain," I said.

Quickly, omitting the variety of small detail, I told them about the hypnosis and its results.

"This is—*true?*—" asked Mrs. Sentas incredulously when I'd finished.

"If you wish you can call Dr. Porter for verification," I told her.

"I may do that," she said.

"Well, I never heard such a load o' crap in my life," Sentas spoke up; but his voice lacked his usual blunt assurance.

"I still don't see why you say my sister is—dead," said Mrs. Sentas.

"I said I *think* she is," I answered. "That's why I asked you if you'd heard from her. The fact that you haven't . . ."

"You're telling us that what you've seen is her—*ghost*?" she asked contemptuously.

"I think it is," I said. I didn't look at Anne.

"I trust you—"

"Come on!" Sentas said.

"I trust you realize what you're asking us to believe," Mrs. Sentas repeated, stiffly.

"I realize it," I said. "But it's your sister I've seen. I'm sure of it now."

"How do you know it was her?" asked Mrs. Sentas. "Assuming you saw anything—which I doubt."

I told her about the dress, about Elizabeth verifying me.

"You saw this?" she whispered. "In *here*?"

"Oh, for chrissake!" Sentas broke in. "He saw a picture o' Helen and he's tryin' t'pull somethin' on us! What d'ya—!"

"Pull *what*, Mr. Sentas?" I interrupted, coldly. "Just what have I to gain by telling you these things?"

He started to answer, then checked himself and glared at me. I turned back to his wife.

"When did your sister leave California?" I asked her.

"Last September," she answered.

"I don't mean to pry," I said, "but—did she have any special reason?"

She shook her head. "No, she did not."

"She didn't act—strangely when she left?"

"We didn't see her leave, Mr. Wallace."

The words acted on me like an electric shock. I stared at her. "I don't understand," I said.

"She just left us a note," said Mrs. Sentas.

I tried to hold back the thunderous beating of my heart.

"I see," I said. "Well . . . shall we try to—?" I gestured toward the card table and chairs.

"Come on, Mildred, let's get the hell outa here," Sentas said.

She waved his words aside, looking at me intently. "What do you hope to accomplish, Mr. Wallace?" she asked. "I may as well tell you I don't believe a word of this talk. But I am concerned about Helen."

"It's very simple," I said. "We sit around that card table and I try to—locate your sister, so to speak."

"Oh, for—!" Sentas stood up with a heavy thump. "Maybe you're crazy enough t' stay here, Mildred, but I ain't!"

"We'll stay." It was all she said but, in a second, I sensed the entire relationship between her and Sentas: the ignorant, loud-mouthed man married to the ugly but well-to-do woman; the woman preferring this to sterile spinsterhood.

I stood up. "Shall we sit down then?" I suggested.

Without a word, Anne and Mrs. Sentas took their places at the table. Mrs. Sentas sat very stiffly, her face an emotion-stripped mask. With a muttered curse, her husband sat across from me, the chair creaking beneath his bulk. He crossed his arms and looked balefully at me. There was something animal in his eyes—and in his mind. I felt waves of it buffeting at me, cold with animosity.

"All right," I said, trying to ignore him, "just sit quietly, please."

Mrs. Sentas didn't move. Anne looked at me fearfully and shuddered. Sentas leaned back in the chair and it squeaked. "Lota crap," he muttered.

Then it was silent. I waited until they were settled fully and closed my eyes. The only sound I could hear was the heavy breathing of Harry Sentas. I tried to blank my mind, feeling positive that something was going to happen. I don't know why I felt so sure; it was just a conviction in my mind.

After a while I began to wonder why Sentas was

breathing so hard. Until, abruptly, with a last fleck of consciousness, I realized that it was me. My chest was laboring with breath and clouds of darkness were settling over my mind. I felt my feet and ankles, hand and wrists going ice cold. My breath grew heavier yet, until it was a violent, body-wrenching intake and output of air. I caught a momentary vision of the three of them staring at me. Then I was gone.

Anne told me later what happened.

Almost as soon as I closed my eyes my breathing became agitated. My head went limp on my neck and lolled from side to side; my hands which started on my lap slid off and hung limply, twitching once in a while; my features went slack, mouth slipping open, all my features losing definition, becoming plastic and devoid of personality.

This went on for many minutes.

Then, suddenly, the accelerated breathing stopped and it was dead quiet.

They gasped as my head snapped up alertly, eyes still shut. There was a dry clicking in my throat, a rattling, a gagging crackle—like the sound of an idiot attempting speech.

Which speech came.

"Mildred," I said, flatly, expressionlessly.

Mrs. Sentas gasped and cringed in her chair, her dark eyes fixed to my face.

"Mildred," I said. "Mildred."

There was a quick, dry exhalation from her.

"You—you'd better answer," Anne told her in a whisper.

*"Mildred?"* I insisted.

". . . yes," she said.

My face fell abruptly into an expression of utter despair. *"Mildred,"* I said, my voice breaking with emotion. "Oh, God, Mildred. Where *are* you?"

"Oh . . ." Mrs. Sentas was trembling, staring at me in horror.

I stretched out my hand. "Mildred?"

"No," she whimpered, drawing back.

"Mildred?" I reached around for her.

"God damn it, stop it," muttered Sentas.

I touched her cold, shaking hand and held it. Mrs. Sentas moaned. She tried to draw it back but I wouldn't let her.

"I'm sorry, Mildred," I said, miserably. "Oh, God, I'm so sorry, darling."

A wild-eyed Sentas started to reach out but Anne held up a hand and blocked him. "No!" she whispered furiously.

"Mildred," I said, "it's me, Helen."

Mrs. Sentas suddenly bent over, sobbing helplessly.

"Mildred, don't hate me," I said, "please don't hate me."

"Stop this damn—!"

Sentas broke off abruptly as, with a serpentlike hiss, I jerked back my hand and sat erect in my chair. Suddenly, my eyes opened.

I stared at him.

"Come on, let's go," he said to his wife, apparently thinking I was now awake.

*"Harry,"* I said in a terrible voice.

He glared at me. "Look, boy," he started, then was quiet, staring at me, open-mouthed, suddenly realizing that I wasn't awake at all.

"Harry," I said, "Harry Sentas." My teeth clenched and breath began to hiss between my teeth. "God damn you to hell, Harry, you dirty bastard, you. You filthy son-of-a—"

Suddenly, I closed my eyes and threw a hand over my eyes. *"Oh, God what have I done?"* I sobbed. I raised my head. I held out imploring hands toward Harry

Sentas, my cheeks covered with running tears.

"Harry, why?" I asked. "Why, Harry, *why*?"

With a hoarse shout, Harry Sentas flung the table over me, sending me sprawling back on the floor.

# TWENTY

I CAME TO WITH A VIOLENT RUSH. SIGHT and sound broke over me like club blows: Sentas starting toward me, face mottled with hate, his wife holding him back; Anne pushing up from her chair to help me; the room spinning and wavering around me. There was a terrible dryness in my throat and upper chest as if those areas had been blotted of all moisture. My head ached pulsingly.

"Honey!" I stared at Anne's fear-distended face as she knelt by me.

"Lemme go!" I heard Sentas snarling. "Who the hell does he think he is, pullin' a stunt like this!"

And Mrs. Sentas' voice, near hysterical, telling him, "Stop it! *Stop it!*"

I couldn't follow the transition from their struggle in the living room to their exit from the house. Time and movement ran together crazily. I thought they were there and then they weren't. I thought I was on the floor and then I was lying on the sofa with Anne bending over me, patting at my face with a cold, wet cloth.

"Water." It was the first thing I managed to say. I sounded like a legionnaire discovered in the desert, dry-lunged and hoarse. I asked for it again and I must have looked terrible because Anne ran into the kitchen and brought back one of the big brown glasses filled with water. I drank it in one convulsive swallow.

Then I sighed and sank back. "Gawd," I said, "I forgot about that one."

"What?" She still looked frightened.

I patted her hand, smiling feebly. "I'm all right," I said. "I forgot about mediums' getting violently thirsty. Not that I'd planned on conking out like that. What in God's name happened?"

She told me.

"No wonder they left," I said.

"With a bang," she said. She shook her head with a pained smile. "This has been one *hell* of a summer," she said.

I returned an equally pained smile and we held on to each other. There wasn't much humor left in us, though. I could feel that old gnawing half-terror, half-awe coming back again.

"Anne," I said.

"Don't say it," she said.

I swallowed. "All right," I agreed, "but—about Sentas."

She drew back, looking worried. "You sure made him angry."

"I think I know why," I said.

She didn't ask the question but I knew she was thinking it.

"Helen Driscoll never went back east," I said.

"She—?" Anne stared at me, waiting.

"She died here," I said. "Sentas killed her."

*"What?"*

"I'd bet on it," I said. "It all fits. If he knew she was back east why should it bother him so much? What happened tonight, I mean."

"Well, I . . . sort of—"

"What, honey?"

"I thought maybe he'd—been having an affair with this Helen Driscoll and was afraid you knew about it and were trying to blackmail him or something. I don't think he believes what you said about the—the medium business."

"I don't think so either," I said, "but his reaction was too strong if it's only what you think—which I think too, of course. I believe he *was* sleeping with Helen Driscoll. But I also believe that he killed her, then wrote that note to make it look as if she'd gone back east, to New York."

"But—where is she then?"

"Probably buried in some canyon," I said.

Anne shuddered. "How *awful*," she said. "But . . . how can we be sure? If she is dead, how can the police prove anything?" I sensed that she was talking quickly to keep to the surface details, avoiding that plunge into the significance of Helen Driscoll's being dead yet being seen and heard.

"I don't know," I said. "I'm sure any testimony I gave would be laughed out of court."

"If only they knew where this woman was buried," Anne said, "assuming you're right—and I'm half inclined to believe it." She shuddered again. "Oh, God," she said. "And he was here—going for you."

"Shhh." I put my arms around her and patted her back. I tried to think of an answer. But what I'd said was perfectly true. What could I tell the police that could, possibly, convince them? *I'm a medium and the murdered woman appeared to me in a vision?* They *would* laugh me out of court. They wouldn't even let me in court in the first place; they'd laugh me out of the station house.

And yet I knew it was true. I knew it. Everything pointed to it. The reaction Sentas had shown to Richard's speaking his name that night. The reaction he'd shown to what I'd said tonight. His obvious attempts to keep his wife away from our house lest she discover anything. The note supposedly left by Helen Driscoll. The fact that her sister had never seen her leave. The basic situation itself—an ugly, dictatorial wife, an animal-like husband; and, finishing the picture, the wife's good-looking sister living in the next house— probably threatening to tell about Sentas' infidelity; the fury rushing to Sentas' brain, his wild little eyes looking for something to hurt with, to—

"I'll be damned," I said.

"What?"

"The poker," I said. I went over to it and, bracing myself, picked it up.

Anne saw the way I twitched. "This is why I left it on the floor that night," I told her. "It's—" Gingerly, I let it drop. "That's what she was killed with," I said.

Anne looked at me, at the poker.

"Bring it over here to the lamp, will you?" I asked.

"Do I—have to?"

"I can't touch it, honey," I said.

As if it were a snake, she brought it over and held it under the bright aura of the lamp.

"I figured as much," I said.

"What?"

"He scrubbed it off. I'm sure there isn't a speck of evidence on it."

Anne grimaced, knowing exactly what I meant by evidence; I could see it in her mind. She put the poker back in its holder as I stood staring into the fireplace.

"Wouldn't there be some other evidence?" she asked.

"It's probably all gone by now. I wouldn't even know where to start looking."

"If it's true," Anne said, "couldn't they—*make* him tell?"

I shook my head. "Without the body it wouldn't mean a—"

It hit me. *"I wonder,"* I said.

She didn't speak but I saw fear creeping back into her face.

"Those old stories," I said, "about—ghosts, about the haunting of houses. They very often find, buried underneath the houses—"

*"Tom."* She looked sick. "For pity's sake."

"I'm sorry," I said. "I know it's a hideous thought but—well it might be true, Anne. That look on the woman's face. Pleading."

"Tom, please . . ."

"Well, there's only one way to find out."

"No," she murmured; then, repelled, added, "Now?"

"Sentas may leave, Anne. If he thinks I have anything definite against him he might get out."

"Yes, but—" She sank down heavily on the sofa. "I can't help you," she said. She shook her head. "Oh God, I hope this is all a dream," she said. "If I find out we've been living on top of a—" She closed her eyes.

"I'll only be a few minutes," I said. I started for the kitchen.

"Tom?"

I turned in the doorway.

"Where . . . where are you going to look?" she asked.

I gestured weakly. "Under the house I guess," I said. "He wouldn't have—done it in the back yard. It might get dug up accidentally."

I looked at her pained expression a moment, then

turned away. "I'll be right back," I said.

I went out into the cold night air and down the alley to the side door of the garage. Inside, I flicked on the light and found the hand shovel—it would be too confined under the house to use the long-handled one. I pulled the battery lantern off its hook and went outside again.

It was no wonder Anne felt as she did, I thought as I moved into the back yard. The idea that we might have been living for more than two months above the grave of a bludgeoned woman was not a pretty one.

There was no cellar; you rarely find one in a California tract house. There was only a small concrete half wall by the hose outlet pipe and an opening just big enough to squeeze through. Letting down the lantern and shovel, I pulled out the metal-framed screen and leaned it against the house. Then I switched on the lantern, grabbed the small shovel and crawled under the house.

It was like a refrigerator under there. The sandy ground was cold and damp. I played the beam of the lantern around, feeling a loosening of relief with every added moment that revealed only flat, untouched earth.

It didn't last. With a start, my arm froze; the white beam of light held on a tiny mound of earth. I felt my heartbeat quicken to a slow, dragging thud. My immediate instinct was to back out fast and leave, tell the police, let them see what was there.

Then I knew I couldn't. It might, after all, be something else. The house was not old. Its builders might have buried some trash there—plaster, wood scraps, bits of cement.

Swallowing, I crawled toward the mound; and, as I did, the doubt began to fade in me. Because it seemed as if I heard someone speak a word in my mind and the word was *yes*.

It was very cramped by the mound and I had to lie almost prone as I dug. In the silence the only sound was the sprinkling thud of the wet, brown earth as I tossed it aside. I tried to ignore the rising pulse of awareness in my mind. Hurry, it seemed to say, *hurry*. I held myself back. I'll be glad when this is over, I told myself, glad when we can return to a semblance of normal living. Perhaps I could find a legitimate medium who could teach me to control this ability completely, this "wild talent." Then it couldn't hurt us, then I could—

A retching sound tore from my lips and I lay staring at the hand I had uncovered.

Little flecks of dirt were skittering from the edges of the hole and bouncing from the fingers. I couldn't take my eyes from them.

Abruptly, then, I plunged the shovel blade into the earth and backed off as quickly as I could. "All right," I mumbled. "All right, it's done. It's done." Now there was the proof and it was done.

Outside, I stood quickly and brushed off my shirt and trousers. I put back the screen, then walked to the kitchen door, turning off the lantern.

In the kitchen I put the lantern on the table. Anne turned quickly in the living room and looked in at me. She didn't say a word. I went in.

"Oh," I said, surprised, "hello, Elizabeth." She was sitting in the green chair wearing her topcoat. She nodded once.

"I told Elizabeth to come over if she felt lonely," Anne said. It was only something to say to fill time, I knew. There was only one thing on her mind.

"Well . . ." I glanced at Elizabeth. "Have you— told—?"

"No."

Elizabeth was staring at my clothes. I looked down and saw that they were stained by the wet earth.

"Well, did you find anything?" Anne blurted suddenly.

I swallowed. "She's down there," I said.

"Oh, God."

There was a rustle from the other side of the room. "So," I heard Elizabeth say.

When I turned, she was pointing the Luger at me.

# TWENTY-ONE

"LIZ, WHAT ARE YOU—" ANNE GOT NO
farther. She stared blankly at the pistol.

I stood without a word looking at Elizabeth's pale,
tension-sick face. For all my talk, I thought; for all my
celebrated awareness, I was as astounded by this as if
I'd never sensed a thing.

"Liz, what is this?" Anne said.

Elizabeth's eyes were terrible to look at.

"You," I said, incredulously, *"you?"*

*"Don't you talk to me like that,"* Elizabeth said; and I
twitched as her finger started to tense on the trigger.

"Elizabeth?" Anne didn't understand. It was obvious by the confused, distraught sound in her voice.

"You had to meddle, didn't you?" Elizabeth said
to me. "Had to meddle."

"Elizabeth," I said, "put . . . put that gun away."

"You'd like that, wouldn't you?" she said. "You'd
like it if the police had taken it away from me. But

they didn't—because Frank said it was an accident. Wasn't that nice of him?" All the contempt and hatred she'd been repressing for months seemed to edge her voice.

"What *is* this?" Anne demanded to know.

"May I sit down?" I asked Elizabeth.

"May you sit down," she echoed scornfully. "What's the difference what you do?"

I sat down slowly so the movement wouldn't startle her. I put my hand over Anne's.

"Liz?" asked my wife.

"Don't you make a pretty picture," said Elizabeth, ignoring her. "A pretty picture." It started as scorn but ended in almost a sob.

"Elizabeth, put that gun—"

"Shut up!" A tear sped down her cheek but she didn't seem to notice it. "I don't want to hear anything from you."

"Elizabeth, what is it?" Anne asked, still not knowing.

"Elizabeth is the—" I started to tell Anne.

"Stop whispering!" Elizabeth ordered.

"Liz, you'll wake up—" Anne broke off as, with a bolt of panic, I squeezed her hand sharply.

"—Richard?" finished Elizabeth, her eyes glittering. "Your *baby*?"

I heard Anne gasp in a breath of air. "What . . . ?" she murmured.

"Tell us about it, Liz," I said, quickly. "If we can help we'll—"

"*Help*—" Her laugh was a sick, convulsive sound. "You're going to help me? You're going to give me back my baby? You are?"

I swallowed dryly. "No, Elizabeth," I said, "but we can help you with the police."

She sat up straight in the chair, the skin tightening across her bloodless cheeks.

"You'll never see the police," she said. "You'll never see anyone. You're a meddler. A damn meddler. I heard you when the Sentas' were here. I heard. I was outside on the porch. I heard. Damn *meddler*—!" Her voice broke again and she drew in a rasping breath to hold back the sob.

"Elizabeth . . ." Only a faint sound from my wife.

"You'd like to know how I killed her, wouldn't you?" said Elizabeth. "How I killed that—*bitch*!"

The word coming from her lips sounded hideous.

"That's what she was," she said. "She didn't care. No, she didn't care. It was al-always open season on men for her. Always. Any man. Any one. Even husbands, *any* husband."

I heard Anne sob slightly. Good old Frank, I thought, good old, *good* old Frank.

"It wasn't—wasn't enough she was stealing her own s-sister's husband," Elizabeth said. "No, n-no, that wasn't enough." The gun wavered in her hand. "She had to branch out, had to get some other husbands too. *Any one*, any one would do. So long as they'd—*get in her filthy bed with her*." Elizabeth spoke the last words through clenched teeth, her body trembling with mindless fury.

"Liz," I started but she paid no attention.

"I found out," she said, nodding, "I found out. Everybody thinks I'm so—so stupid. Poor old Liz. *P-p-poor old Liz*. Doesn't know a thing, not a thing. Poor old Liz. Just—just a stupid old—" Another gasped-in sob shook her body.

I started up.

"Sit down!" she shouted fiercely; I shrank back quickly. She glared at me and it was obvious there was not much left in her that was sane. It was little wonder after what she'd been through.

"I found out," she went on, nodding, a terrible, humorless smile on her lips, "I found out. Frank thought I didn't know but I did. That's why he let me have a baby. You didn't know that, did you? I had to bargain for it. I had to make a bargain—"

Suddenly, her free hand clutched across her cheek and one eye. "With my own husband I had to make a bargain so I could have a baby! That's wonderful, isn't that w-w-wonderful?"

"Liz, don't," I muttered. It was sickening to listen to her pitiful voice spilling out all the horrors she'd had to live with.

"Oh, you're going to hear all of it," she said, extending the Luger toward us. I pressed close to Anne, ready to jump in front of her if I had to. "*Every single dirty detail* of it," she said.

She sank back against the chair.

"Frank went out that night, I don't know where. Who cares where he went? Probably out with some girl, with some cheap—" She stopped and shuddered fitfully, lips pressed together, her face the mask of a demented woman.

"I saw Sentas come over here," she said. "His wife was out. So he came—*creeping over here.*" Her voice was a contemptuous whine. "Like a dog who smelled the air and knew there was a *bitch* around."

Little Elizabeth; shy, quiet Elizabeth.

"He wasn't here long," she said. "It didn't take them long. Then he came out. The house was dark so I went over. The door wasn't locked. And I went in.

"She wasn't in the living room. I knew she wouldn't be. There was only one place she'd be, one place her kind would be. Lying on a bed. So I—I—" She seemed breathlessly excited at the memory. "I picked up the poker—that one over there; you didn't know that, did you? And I went in the bedroom."

It was deathly still in the room—except for the harsh breathing of Elizabeth Wanamaker, who had wanted only to have a baby and be loved.

"She was still dressed," she said, her voice hard and savage. "She still had her dress on. The black one!" she said to me, smiling for an instant; awfully. "The one you asked me about, remember? With—with the Aztec symbols on it? She hadn't even taken it off." Her voice was a hating whine again. "She'd just pulled it up over her hips. That's all! That's all she needed. Pull it up like a—like a—"

She flung a talon of a hand over her eyes again and there was a horrible sob in her chest, racking her. "Oh, God!" she cried, "Oh, *God*! I killed her and I'd kill her again! Again and again and again and again and again!" A line of spittle ran across her jaw. She didn't even notice it.

She sat there, panting.

"I killed her," she recalled with renewed relish, "I hit her on the head while she was lying down. She got up and I hit her again. She fell on the floor. I hit her again. She crawled into the hall and I went after her. I hit her again. She crawled into the living room. I hit her again. I hit her again. I hit her again. I hit her again."

She went on and on in a mechanical voice, droning the same four words. Until, suddenly, she stopped and looked at us.

"So," she said, "aren't you surprised, Anne? Surprised what your little Liz can do? What she can do to *bitches*? And to husbands who sleep with bitches?"

"Elizabeth." Anne couldn't look at her. She lowered her eyes and closed them.

"Elizabeth," I said.

She looked at me.

"Listen," I said. "Let us help you. You're not well, Liz. No one is going to punish you for something you did when you weren't well. You—"

"Well!" she said, half speaking the word, half laughing it. "Not well! *Oh*. Oh, aren't you bright? Aren't you brilliant? I'm not well. Isn't that smart of you."

She leaned forward, deadly calm again, with that sudden mad reversal of mood.

"I don't care what happens to me," she said. "You understand? *I don't care*. I lost my baby. I lost it. I can't have any more. I lost my husband, I don't want any more. I killed a woman—a bitch. I tried to kill a man. You think I care what happens to me now? You think anything could hurt me now? *Do* you?"

"Do you want to hurt more, Eliz—"

"Yes!" she flared, her lips twisting back from clenched teeth. "Yes, I want to hurt! I want to hurt! I want to make other people know what it is to—to—to *suffer*! I want to make people know!"

"Elizabeth, if you put that gun down, nothing will happen to you," I said. "If you don't—"

"Nothing will happen!" she cried, laughing again, louder. "God, you're funny! Oh, *God*, you're so funny!"

"Mama?"

We were all statues at the sound. I felt my heart leap in my chest like a thing alive. Anne gasped, then was soundless. Elizabeth's eyes darted toward the hallway.

Suddenly she lurched to her feet. *"Yes!"* she said.

"No!" I was up and blocking her way before I knew what I was doing. With a deranged cry, Elizabeth flung up the pistol and fired. Anne screamed; and something smashed across my skull and sent me flailing back with a grunt. I felt myself falling; then, driven only by instinct, I was on my knees trying to stand, something hot and wet running across my right eye. I saw Elizabeth lunge for the hallway and I dove at her, my nails raking over her shoes.

Suddenly, a piercing shriek ballooned the walls of the house. I slapped at the hot liquid gushing over my eyes, falling back against the sofa.

Elizabeth came backing from the hallway, an expression of utter terror on her face.

"No," she mumbled. "No. No."

She stumbled and caught herself, her eyes following something. *Something that moved after her.* I couldn't see anything but I suddenly knew what it was. I heard Richard crying.

"Get away," Elizabeth said, her voice a hollow, inhuman sound. "Get away . . ."

Her heel twisted under her and she fell back. A scream tore apart her lips. "Get away!" she howled. She jerked up the pistol and fired at the air; the explosion rocking deafeningly through the room. Richard screamed. With a choking, gagging sound, Elizabeth scuttled back one-handedly across the rug, saliva threading across her shaking jaw.

"No," she cried. Abruptly, she raised the Luger to her own head and pulled the trigger. There was a clicking sound as the hammer hit the empty chamber. She pulled the trigger again, again; in vain. Then, with a wail of absolute terror, her eyes rolled back and her head thudded heavily on the floor.

I sat staring at her lying there. Anne bent over me, her eyes wide with fright.

"S'all right," I mumbled. "Take care Richard . . ."

Then I was in the night.

I came to in an unfamiliar bed. Anne was sitting nearby, looking at me anxiously. As my eyes fluttered open, she took my hand.

"You're all right?" she asked.

"Sure." I blinked and looked around. "Where are we?"

"Inglewood," she said. "In the hospital."

"Oh." Then I remembered. "How's Richard?" I asked.

"He's fine," she said. "He's outside in the waiting

room. Some nurse has taken a fancy to him; she's reading him a story."

"Thank God," I said. "When Liz started for the—" I grunted as a dull wave of pain ran across my head. "What happened to me?" I asked.

"A bullet grazed your head," she said.

"Bad?"

"No; the doctor says it'll be fine." She leaned over and kissed me. "Lordy, I was scared," she murmured.

I kissed her cheek. "How's the wee one?" I asked.

"Still in there," she said, "though God only knows why."

I chuckled weakly. "The way things have been going," I said, "she'll never want to come out."

She smiled, then squeezed my hand tightly. "I'll always remember how you stood up and faced that gun to save Richard," she said.

"I didn't do a very good job," I said. "It took Helen Driscoll to save him."

"You think . . . ?"

"Of course," I said. "Elizabeth saw her. Can't understand why *I* didn't, though. Say, where is she?"

"In a prison hospital," she said.

"That poor kid." I sighed. For some reason I remembered that comb; and realized that the *death* I'd sensed had been that of Helen Driscoll. I didn't know but I'd have bet that Elizabeth had had the comb in her pocket the night she killed Helen Driscoll. Killed her so brutally in the darkness that Helen Driscoll never knew who had murdered her but thought it was her brother-in-law.

*Even afterward.*

"And I went over and asked Elizabeth questions about it," I said, remembering the fear and suspicion in her mind. "What a medium," I said.

"You—think you still are?" Anne asked.

"I don't know," I said.

\*　　\*　　\*

But I wasn't. I don't know what happened—unless that head wound joggled something in my brain. Or maybe I'd only had the power limitedly—or for a specific purpose. At any rate it's gone.

But I can always say I batted a thousand in my predictions. Because, in late September, Anne went to the hospital and, after delivery, I visited her and she asked me in a sweet little doped-up voice, "Was it a girl?"

I kissed her and grinned.

"What else?" I said.

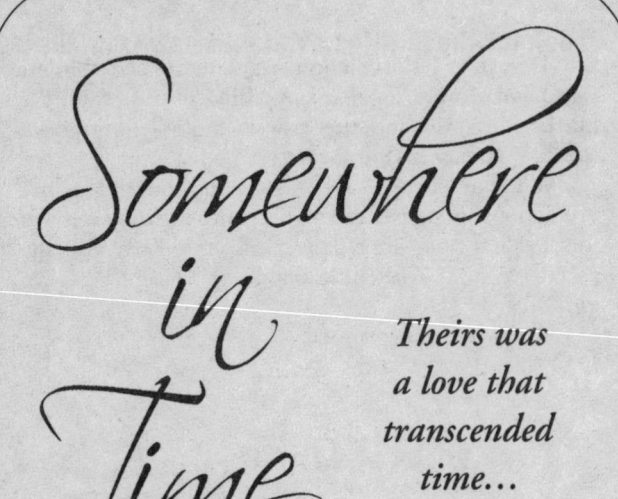

# *Somewhere in Time*

*Theirs was
a love that
transcended
time...*

# Richard Matheson

A modern man whose love for a woman he has never met leads him back in time to a luxury hotel in 1896 San Diego. There he finds his soul mate in the form of a celebrated actress of the previous century. This classic novel was the winner of the World Fantasy Award for Best Novel, and adapted for the 1979 movie staring Christopher Reeve and Jane Seymour. *Somewhere in Time* remains a classic romance.

*"Stylish and gripping, [Richard Matheson's] stories not only entertain but touch the mind and heart."* —Dean Koontz

**JULY 2008**
978-0-7653-6139-4 • 0-7653-6139-6

www.tor-forge.com